Felicity's Power

by

J. Arlene Culiner

Felicity's Power

Cover Art by *Kim Mendoza*

The Wild Rose Press, Inc.
PO Box 708
Adams Basin, NY 14410-0708
Visit us at www.thewildrosepress.com

Publishing History
previously published by Power of Love Publishing, Australia, 2001
First *Last Rose Of Summer* Edition, 2015
Print ISBN 978-1-62830-875-4
Digital ISBN 978-1-62830-876-1

Dedication

With thanks to my excellent editor,
Eilidh MacKenzie

"You are old, Father William," the young man said,
"And your hair has become very white;
And yet you incessantly stand on your head—
Do you think, at your age, it is right?"

Lewis Carroll,
Alice's Adventures in Wonderland

"Making a quick getaway?"

Felicity stood in the doorway taking in the scene: the open but fully packed suitcase on the bed, Marek's trench coat flung over the table. He was on his way out. No denying the evidence.

Marek sat in the armchair by the window, his face tight, his eyes haunted. "I'm sitting here, in a chair, right? Aren't the words 'a quick getaway' somewhat of an exaggeration?" He drawled the words out slowly, mockingly.

"Okay then. A slow getaway."

He stared at her, unable to pull his eyes away. Her face was pale, her expression wild. Loose tendrils of hair shadowed her neck, calling attention to the slow throb of veins under the delicate skin. She looked sexy as hell. Tempting and far too dangerous to think about.

"Not quick, not slow. Neither one of the above. No getaway." His voice was icy, impersonal.

"That!" Her arm waved wildly, gesticulated in the direction of the suitcase. A sharp, searing feeling of betrayal mixed with humiliation kept her tense, unrelenting. "I mean, if you want me out of here, all you have to do is tell me. Since you're obviously desperate to get rid of me." She felt as if she'd been stabbed. She crossed the room slowly until she was standing beside him, staring down at him, her eyes flashing with determination and fury. "But let's not forget you were the one who invited me up here. Remember?"

Praise for J. Arlene Culiner

"A great read done with a fun, quirky and different setting. You won't be able to put it down."

~Harlequin Junkie

~*~

"This book definitely falls into my 'feel good romance' category! Loved the story, the characters, the setting...a great choice for those of us in the 'older' population who would like to sit down and enjoy a mature romance with mature characters."

~K&T Book Reviews

~*~

"Gosh, I enjoyed reading this book immensely. If there is love from both sides of a relationship, even against tough odds, things have a way of always turning out right. A heart warming tale when all is said and done."

~Diana Lanos, Smile Somebody Loves You

~*~

"I loved this novel and Culiner's writing is magnificent, the dialogue is magical and masterful. An emotional, heartfelt, dazzling experience. Enjoy!"

~Sheila Clapkin, author of, A Life Story, Dr. Du Bimo

~*~

"Love, lust and longing are here aplenty. Culiner's unerring gift for off-beat characters, her sharp wit and believable dialogue...keep[s] eyes and pulses racing page to page...Gritty, authentic and fun."

~Penny Lynn Cookson

~*~

"The characters are inventive and yet grounded in human truths; the writing is witty and begs to be read over and over again; the story is pristine and poignant."

~Kindah Mardham Bey, Lucid Forge

Chapter One

"You're right, of course. This dream is going to blow sky high, just the way Owen's did a hundred and fifty years ago."

A woman's voice. Rich, throaty. Lazy. Marek Sumner looked up from the lecture notes he'd been shuffling together. Audacious, slanting brown eyes scrutinized him, taking his measure in a leisurely way.

"You must be the only one here who agrees with me," he drawled slowly, stalling for time while his own glance played back over her with the same boldness. His gut tingled, a deep, primitive reaction. Nothing to do with words or ideas.

She tossed her head, scornfully. "I know. I spend my days arguing with people who believe a society of peace and love is possible. That, the 'revolution' will come, and the police will waltz through the streets distributing flowers."

"I'll bet that doesn't make you many friends here in Haight-Ashbury." He kept his voice dry, calm, belying the wild, reckless response teasing the edge his consciousness. Adrenaline had begun pumping, tightening his muscles, his skin.

"Of course it doesn't." Her shrug showed how little "making friends" mattered to her. "It's easy for students to claim material goods don't count. In a few years, when they're career-oriented citizens with families and mortgages, they'll change their minds, all right."

Fascinated, he noted the mass of curling orange hair pulled together in a high, wild knot at the top of her head. *Who are you? Where did you come from?* Tallish, very slender, almost fragile—yet tough as steel. He could certainly sense that. Astounding looking. A sharp thrill rippled along nerves stretched elastic tight.

"Of course they will." He smiled slowly. "Which is why I wanted to give this lecture on the 'Empire of Good Sense.' In 1825, Owen's ideas were radical: common property, equality of the sexes, absolute individual freedom. And, in the end, his commune failed. Just like any hippie 'revolution.' "

The words came automatically. Watching her, he forgot about ideas, time, the room, the people waiting to talk to him, the soft evening sun spilling through the Bookworm's wide doorway. He forgot everything except this woman standing here, right in front of him.

And she knew it. Her secret smile met his. Still the conversation continued, words weaving together, forming a bridge where they could meet.

"I've been called a reactionary three times in the last ten minutes." He laughed.

"The ultimate insult!" She laughed back, a rich warm sound, as smooth as a caress on his bare skin.

"Thank goodness, as a traitor to the people's revolution, I'm more likely to be smothered under a blanket of flower petals than face a firing squad."

"With your detractors all chanting, 'I love you.' " She stopped abruptly, her smile fading, faint shock sliding into her eyes.

I love you. The words—so casually, so mockingly said—had jolted him, too.

2

He stared at her, his excitement pulsing into want. High cheekbones, a thin, slightly aquiline nose. Freckles—childish freckles contradicting the hawk-like ferocity of her features: she was a mixture of Tom Sawyer and a foreign queen. Dancing brown eyes that probed, tempted, provoked. This was a woman certain of her charms, of her magnetism. And aware of her power to seduce him.

He also knew he was having the identical effect on her, and the amused and softened curve of her mouth also showed him she wasn't considering a refusal. An austere, elegant mouth. Narrow lips. Difficult to pull his eyes away from them…

Then, as quickly as it started, it was over.

Myra had suddenly appeared at his side, touched his arm possessively. Her voice was cool, assured. "Marek, Professor Lyle wants to speak to you about Owen. And Mike Evans needs to give you details about the anti-war protest on Saturday." She hadn't even given the red-haired woman a glance. But Marek hadn't been fooled. He knew Myra well, very well indeed. Her movements had been too deliberate, her voice too controlled. She'd been very conscious of the other woman's presence. Had she also been aware of the intensity of Marek's interest?

Professor Lyle? He didn't care what Lyle had to say. Not now. He didn't want to go talk to Mike Evans either. He wanted to stay here, right here, beside this woman with the glorious, wild mane of hair. He wanted to know what her skin would feel like. He wanted to know the pressure of her mouth as he covered it with his own, the heat of her body when he took her in his arms. Yet he couldn't expect Myra to just vanish, could he? Or tell her he wanted to be left alone with an unknown woman who glowed like a hot ember.

Myra took his hand in hers.

"Excuse me," he murmured, regretfully. Allowed Myra to tow him away. He felt foolish, like a poodle on a leash led by an imperious mistress. He glanced back, briefly. The brown eyes mocked him, he, a mere show dog, being pulled into the ring.

Professor Lyle was waiting, a rabid expression visible on his own bulldog face. Once again, Marek was thrust into the heat of the debate, but he no longer felt the slightest interest in Owen and his experimental community. He muttered perfunctory answers, nodded complacently at the barrage of argument. Then looked around, his eyes scanning the room, searching for that hair, the pale, knowing face. He would break away, find her again. Talk to her. The need was imperative.

She'd gone. Vanished. No doubt about it—she'd stand out in any crowd. He felt a deep, dragging sense of disappointment. For what? Immediate desire, instant fascination? That was all.

Idiot. Those emotions were banal, superficial, despite their intensity. Unnecessary, up-rooting responses. *Forget it.* He'd probably never see the woman again.

****

This memory you're dragging out is forty-three years old!

The thought stopped Marek Sumner in his tracks. Forty-three years? His mind went completely blank.

The sun shimmered down at him, just the way it had on that spring day, long ago. Sun? Was his memory playing tricks on him? Fooling him. Touching the long-finished romance with a glittery foil brilliance. Spring in San Francisco usually meant fog, gray skies.

And it was time he opened his eyes. This wasn't 1971. So many years had passed. This was summer, and he was now sixty-five years old. Things had changed in this city.

What an eager young man he'd been when he'd left here in 1976, heading east for his first teaching post, freshly won doctorate in hand. He tried to drum up a memory of that young Marek, and a wry smile twitched at his lips. How intense he'd been, serious, determined to succeed. An idealist, a man with a mission.

Had he succeeded? Well…more or less. Not in everything, of course. He rolled out the list. There had been the professorship in Boston, the books he'd written—critical analyses of contemporary literature—before taking the frightening leap into creative non-fiction writing. These days, the name Marek Sumner was almost a household word. So much for positives. On the negative side, was his marriage to Nathalie, his subsequent divorce. But the birth of Daniel brought him back to positives again. Good. More on the positive side than on the negative.

Still, he wondered what the eager young man he'd once been would think about a life which had been, for all intents and purposes, so calm. That young Marek had wanted to move mountains, but after a few years out in the world, he'd learned that although you could nibble at them with dynamite and machinery, mountains stayed. And wisdom trotted in, told you to get on with your real work and leave mountains alone.

Marek shook his head as if to clear it of ghosts he should have vanquished a long time ago. Ordering his legs to get moving, he turned the corner. The Haight had certainly changed. Back in the sixties and seventies, the streets had been filled with people: dropouts, students, children, musicians, idealists, dreamers, hangers on. There had been protest, noise, talk of revolution, flowers, colorful clothes, and music.

"And yet it's all so conformist! We all think we're being original, but we're really only carbon copies!" Felicity's voice was still there in his head. Felicity protesting, railing, fuming. "Everything should be challenged, questioned. Everything! Every idea!"

Then she'd vanished in a puff of smoke.

Nowadays chic, expensive-looking boutiques replaced the seedy storefronts. Well-heeled, imitation flower children window-shopped. The Bookworm still straddled the corner of Haight and Ashbury, but any similarity ended there. The tiny shop was gone. What was once a haven for burgeoning poets and writers had expanded, become a bookstore with a flourishing international business.

Well, what had he expected? Marek laughed at himself. When you came back on a pilgrimage, you couldn't expect to fall into a time warp where everything had remained the same. That would be asking for the impossible.

Automatic, plate glass doors slid open with a subtle hum. He stared. Once upon a time, a tattered, green velvet sofa had sent out a leisurely invitation from there, the alcove on the left. Where had the brown wooden benches gone? The scarred worktables that had vied for space with chaotic bookshelves?

All vanished. Existing only in the dimension of memory now.

Those contemporary, experimental paintings on the wall, psychedelic posters, the coffee machine? The speaker's pew? These days there were cashiers, other efficient-looking employees. People evidently came to the Bookworm to buy books, not to while away sunny afternoons weaving dreams of change.

Marek marched up to one of the cashiers and asked for Carl Hewlett.

"You're Marek Sumner, aren't you?" The young, gentle-looking woman smiled up at him. She was exceptionally pretty, he noted.

"I suppose I am." He smiled back.

"I recognized you from the photo on your book jacket." She picked up a telephone. "He's here!" She couldn't keep the edge of admiration out of her voice.

In less than a minute, a short, round man was propelling his way through the store.

"Marek!" Carl's face was rosy with pleasure as he clasped Marek's hands in his own.

"Carl. I'd recognize you anywhere! You've hardly changed." No, that wasn't quite true. In the old days, Carl had been a stocky person with a black beard, long black hair and a shiny, grinning face. He was still stocky—even more so. A belt buckle was entirely responsible for holding up his vast belly, and the added pounds made his legs look even shorter. The face was the same, though: round, red, good-natured. He still wore his hair and beard long, but both had turned a bright, pure white. No longer a revolutionary, Carl had evolved into an entrepreneurial Santa Claus.

"When did your plane get in? Why didn't you call and tell me when you were arriving? I'd have picked you up at the airport." There was hurt accusation in

Carl's eyes.

Marek gripped his shoulder fondly. "It's okay. I arrived just a few hours ago. I checked into the hotel, left my bags. I didn't need to be picked up. I suppose I wanted to get used to being here again. Walk around the city." He smiled. "Take a little stroll down memory lane."

"Why have you waited so long?"

"I didn't mean to let all the years slide by like that. They just did."

Carl grinned up at him with complicity. "I know the feeling. Funny how time goes by at a snail's pace when you're a kid sitting in a school classroom, then speeds up crazily after you hit fifty."

"You call it funny?"

Carl led Marek into his office. At least here some of the old chaos reigned. A desk was piled high with books and papers. Cartons vied for place with magazines, empty cups, a computer, briefcases, and several potted plants grown so large, they could never be moved.

"I hate to admit this," said Carl. "Marek, you're looking good. Too good. How have you managed to retain all that well-muscled grace of yours? Even the charisma's still in place; you could charm snakes away from a fakir." Carl sighed. "It just isn't fair."

Marek grinned, took a seat. "You should talk. You're the one married to a woman who's twenty-two years younger."

"And a great fan of yours. Beware!" Carl threw a mock warning across the desk. "So how does it feel to be back in the old stomping ground?"

"Not entirely comfortable," said Marek, slowly.

"Perhaps it's better to let memories stay unchallenged. They're often sweeter than reality was."

Carl had caught the regretful note. "That sounded strangely bitter."

"Did it? It shouldn't have. Wistful, perhaps." But his departure all those years ago had also had a tinge of bitterness about it. And the emotion seemed to have hung on.

"I hope you don't mind, but quite a few of the old crowd will be here for the book signing. They were thrilled to hear you were coming back."

"You still keep in touch with some of them?"

"They're still clients." Carl chuckled. "Only the couch potatoes are in hiding."

The old crowd: Marek forced himself to look cheerful, but he wasn't feeling overly enthusiastic. Did he really want to see everyone again? One person, yes: Felicity Powers. But that was impossible.

"Who's coming?"

"Myra, definitely. You remember your old flame Myra, don't you?" Carl beamed. "Of course, she's been married for the last thirty-odd years. Her husband became one of the cleverest corporate lawyers in the city. Then there's Danny Tobias, Jenny Catten, Libbet, and John Crandon just to name a few. I wonder if you'll recognize them all."

"I doubt it," said Marek shaking his head. "It could even be embarrassing when I don't. I've been meeting so many people for so many years, quite a few of them seem to have slipped out of my memory."

"I suppose you'll be forgiven. Famous people usually are."

"Either that, or they're hounded into the ground,"

Marek answered ruefully. There was one question he really wanted to ask. Just the one. It hovered on his lips, fought to be voiced. He tried to push it down, away, back. Then lost the battle.

"How about Felicity Powers?" He tried to keep his voice light, disinterested sounding, but even to his own ears, it sounded forced. He'd always been a rotten actor, he thought wryly. He'd never learned the fine art of dissimulation.

"Felicity Powers!" Carl gave him a strange look. "You still wondering what happened to her? You asked me about her when we met up in New York over thirty years ago!"

"Did I?" Of course he had—even though he'd been married to Nathalie at the time. "I guess some people have a way of sticking in your mind."

Carl nodded. "I suppose you're right. Felicity was a real beauty back in the old days, wasn't she? Intelligent too. But a bit of a crank. I always thought she was unstable, difficult. I sometimes wonder what she did with her life."

"So do I. But not because she was unstable. She wasn't. Eager, perhaps. Argumentative. And determined to see and experience things. Which is why I wonder how far she got."

"Of course I didn't know her as well as you did." Carl's face showed he didn't consider that such a bad thing. Had Carl also known how badly Felicity's departure had wounded him? Or had he managed to hide the hurt?

"No, she never showed up here again. Funny, everyone thought the two of you made a great couple. Then, suddenly, she was gone."

Disappeared out of his life like a streak of greased lightning. "She wanted to live big, she said." Marek smiled palely. "I can't tell you how many times she told me that underneath my hippie exterior, I was a conservative stuffed shirt."

Carl frowned. "Don't believe it, not even for one minute. If you'd been a conservative stuffed shirt, you never could have written those books."

"Perhaps I've written them *because* I'm such a stuffed shirt."

Carl waved his arm, a gesture of denial. "So when was the last time you saw Felicity? When you went to Paris?"

"Yes, in Paris," Marek confirmed. Paris with Felicity, now that was an old memory. "Back in 1974."

"What the hell was she doing there?"

"Selling roast chestnuts on the street." Marek couldn't repress the grin twitching at his mouth.

"Selling chestnuts? She gave up university to sell chestnuts? Like I said, she was crazy."

"Not really. She didn't have working papers, and the only job she could get was selling on the street. I like to think of Felicity as a survivor more than anything else."

"No doubt she was. Way back then. Nowadays she's most likely married to a nice middle class French businessman, dresses conservatively, dyes her hair, has a permanent, a facelift, and dotes on her grandchildren. Or great-grandchildren!"

"Most likely." Marek chuckled, but to his own ears, it was a forced sound. The thought of a nice normal Felicity didn't give him any pleasure. It was too conventional. He'd wanted Felicity to succeed in the unconventional—but he'd never know if she had.

Carl got to his feet. "Well, Marek, come. I'm taking you home with me now. Liz will never forgive me if I don't. She's been cooking and baking for the last two days."

So the subject of Felicity Powers was dropped. Silently, Marek acknowledged how foolish he'd been, hoping she'd be in San Francisco now. She wasn't. And she would continue being what she'd been for the last forty-odd years: a subtle, fleeting memory. A very faint perfume floating over all the intervening time.

Chapter Two

Felicity Powers virtually grabbed the *International Herald Tribune* out of the flight attendant's hand. Then, feeling the laser beam of hostility shooting in her direction, she looked up meekly.

"Excuse me for acting like a two-year-old with a chocolate bunny. I just got carried away. I haven't read an English language paper for so long." She forced herself to smile brightly, just to show she wasn't really dangerous.

Hesitation flickered in dark exotic eyes, before the attendant moved away.

"Probably thinks she's got a psychopath on board," Felicity muttered to no one in particular. "Who else would get excited reading about wars, revolutions, murders, floods, and earthquakes?"

Outside the cabin window, thin, stringy clouds floated over a lunar landscape. They might be somewhere over Iran at the moment, she reckoned. Somewhere. It all looked so empty down there, so devoid of life. Only the rows of round crater-like water wells hinted at centuries of human occupation. Strange how sitting in a plane always felt like being suspended in time. Isolated from reality. She couldn't begin to count the number of flights she'd taken over the last four decades, but still, this strange feeling never left her.

She opened the newspaper. As expected, there was news of a civil war, a volcano, a series of bombings in the Middle East, a kidnapping, three financial scandals, and a famine. So much misery, and she was turning her back on it. She fought down the spike of guilt searing through her and tried reasoning with herself. She'd given more than thirty years of her life to helping others. She'd put herself in danger so many times, tried to fight battles that had nothing to do with her. She had the right to stop for a while! Take the time to do something else.

Like what? *Write about it.*

What if she was no good at writing?

She pushed the thought out of her mind. How did people know if they were good at anything until they tried? *And failed*, squeaked the little voice inside her head.

Stop it!

She hastily turned to the cultural pages of the paper and began to smile. There were reviews of films she'd never heard of, starring actors and actresses she didn't even know existed. A contemporary artist was showing his work in a New York museum: a critic called it "Jubilant Renunciation"—whatever that was!

As for literature...

She froze.

Marek Sumner's Newest Book
Sophisticated, droll, brilliantly polished.

Here was his photo on the shaking page. No! The pages weren't shaking. Her hands were. She swallowed, stared. He'd cut his hair. *Of course he has, you idiot! You last saw him in 1974.* In the photo, his hair was charmingly tousled, salt and pepper gray. He'd abandoned his wire-rimmed John Lennon glasses, wore elegant framed ones now. And there was the fine nose, that sensual mouth, a determined chin. The face of a poet, he'd had back then when she'd known him. And loved him. Still did have a poet's face.

He looked...wonderful. Damn!

But it was the eyes that drew her, riveted her, and the stream of long buried feeling bubbled up. Deep green eyes, unforgettable eyes, although the black and white image on the printed page in front of her gave no hint of the color. Clear, unwavering eyes, they seemed to be staring straight at her. Almost as if they were sending her a message. Beckoning!

Honestly and truly, Felicity Powers. That could just about take the prize for the stupidest thought you've had today.

Marek. Sending her messages. Ridiculous.

Still, here was his image, turning her inside out. Again. Just the way he had when they'd first met. When she'd, despite her thudding heart, gone up to talk to him. Eyes like a deep, tropical sea. She'd seen the flash of them when she'd walked into the Bookworm and that first glance had her forgetting she'd come there for a book. She forgot everything.

He'd been standing in the middle of a group of people, a tall, pale blonde woman at his side. A beauty. Just the sort of looks considered ideal in those days: hair parted in the middle and falling to her waist, pale blue eyes in a porcelain china face. Felicity had felt the stab of jealousy followed by a wave of rage at her own complexion: the chaotic mass of freckles, the angular starkness of her features, hay-stack hair the color of stewed pumpkin.

15

Turning to her right, she'd asked the closest person to her, a diminutive young woman in torn jeans and tank top, if she knew who he was. "The tall man in the middle of the circle. With glasses. The one with the long hair," she'd added inanely and then wanted to kick herself. Pretty well everyone in the room—male or female—had long hair.

The look of surprise indicated Felicity should, certainly, have known the answer.

"That's Marek Sumner. He's giving the lecture here tonight on Owen."

"Oh," she'd murmured faintly. "A lecture? I didn't know there was one."

The woman threw her a look of pure, open complicity. "He's gorgeous, isn't he?"

Felicity twitched with embarrassment. Had her interest been so transparent? Evidently it had. "If you like the type." She tried to sound bored and blasé. And failed to impress the woman at her side.

"Half the women in the Haight are in love with him."

Of course they would be. What had she expected? He was the sort of man she wanted. A man she wanted to be standing beside. A man she wanted to belong to, to belong to her. If that were the case, it would also be the desire of a lot of other women. Shrugging, she kept her voice cool. "And is he in love with half the women in the Haight?"

"No such luck." The woman chuckled. "Myra's put up private property and no trespassing signs."

"Who's Myra? The blonde?"

"She's gorgeous too, isn't she?" The woman made a wry face.

"Yup." But Felicity wasn't looking at Myra. *Marek Sumner.* The name rode nicely on her heart. She couldn't peel her eyes away from him. "Strange. Normally gorgeous people choose ugly mates."

"Because they don't like the competition?"

"Or because they like the admiration ugliness has for beauty." She probably sounded like sour grapes, and she didn't care.

Both of them had laughed then. And Felicity had stayed, listened to the lecture. There was nothing else she could have done. She wanted to hear the rich, deep tones of his voice. And once she did, she knew she wasn't going anywhere. Not until she'd met him, talked to him, passed a message on to him, somehow—by telepathy if need be—telling him she existed and she wanted him. Just like that, and just that simply.

An hour later, when the lecture was long over, her chance came. Myra had momentarily vanished, the circle around him temporarily thinned. She had to move in fast.

Now! Or never.

Crossing the room like a panther about to sink its fangs into an elk, she approached.

She couldn't remember now what she'd said to him although, to her own ears, her voice had sounded high, squeaky, and ridiculous. No doubt her words hadn't been brilliant either. Her thoughts had been racing too madly for anything coherent to have come out.

He'd raised those green eyes and looked at her. Really looked. It felt like he was touching her all over with that glance, and it almost shocked her. She grew hot, cold, felt less like a predator and more like a rabbit faced by a stoat.

17

Then his mouth had quirked into a smile, an incredible smile, wonderful, thrilling, very sensual, and she knew she had to fight. She heard herself talking from what seemed a million miles away, holding up her end of a perfectly normal conversation.

"Do you often give lectures here?" As far as banal went, this was a corker.

He didn't seem to mind. Instead the eyes were amused as they watched her, searching, measuring. "Never. This is a first."

"Really? But it was fascinating!" Inwardly she winced. What would she come out with next? As if he needed her approval. As if her praise was worth anything.

"Thanks." He actually looked pleased. That wasn't all. Gentle, encouraging. More than that, too. No, this wasn't just any old, polite chit-chat. There was an undercurrent, an undertow, even. He was interested in her, very interested. Tension flickered between them. Elemental response.

His smile was warm, but his gaze was relentless, provocative. "So you don't agree with the people in this room who think we're on the verge of a new society, a revolution?"

"No!" She'd shaken her head violently. "It's ridiculous to believe we'll have a peaceful 'People's Revolution.' That everyone in the country will suddenly know capitalism is wrong and rush into the streets shouting 'I love you.'"

She'd almost stumbled over those three little words and felt the embarrassed flush of red on her cheeks.

I love you.

Out on the street, here in the Haight, people said

that to each other as easily as they said hello. The words had become senseless, a sort of in-crowd identification slogan.

Now, saying them to this man, they changed back again. Took on their old, dark, deep meaning. She wondered what it would feel like to be able to say those very words to him, what it would feel like if he said them back. If he meant them in their original way, the way that could make you ache.

As he looked into her eyes, his mouth quirked in a smile, almost as if he'd caught the thought. As if he were daring her to make the words a reality.

Then Myra, the tall, blonde beauty, had surfaced again, had taken his arm and led him away. She hadn't even thrown her, Felicity, a glance. Hadn't even acknowledged her existence.

But she was aware of her, all right. Her movements had been too deliberate as she led her man to safety, away from the danger she must have sensed, the intensity crackling in the air between them.

Unless she, Felicity, had misinterpreted everything. Unless the smile, that gaze, had only been part of Marek Sumner's natural charisma, the charm handed out to all and sundry. The spell he cast to conquer the hearts of all the women in the Haight.

****

The plane hit an air pocket, bouncing Felicity back into now.

Had she been thinking about Marek Sumner again? For the twenty-millionth time in all the long years! Ridiculous. Marek Sumner had most likely forgotten her very existence. Those days were over. Long gone. Marek was a happily married man—Felicity had seen pictures of his wife years ago in a Paris literary review: a dark-haired woman, elegant, determined. She probably managed Marek's life and career with an iron fist. She would have had to. Marek was too charming, too good-looking.

Felicity looked down at the newspaper still clutched tightly in her hands. Age hadn't changed those looks of his any. Sighing, she plunged into the article.

The praise of Marek's new book was lavish, gushing even. Emphasis was laid upon the fact that he'd spent his youth in California, had studied at the university in San Francisco. Now he was back in town for the first time, for the signing of his book at the Bookworm, for a trip down memory lane.

Felicity blinked. The Bookworm? Did that place still exist? Was it still run by Carl Hewlett? Impossible! Her lips twitched. San Francisco, Carl, Marek. God! It had all been so long ago. The place must have changed so drastically!

She felt a stab of nostalgia. Would it still be there, the feeling? That intensity? If, by chance, one day she came face to face with Marek Sumner? She thought of all the things he'd been. Frank, intelligent. Powerful. An incredible lover. The thought squeezed her heart.

Hard to believe they'd never meet again, that all that feeling had come to nothing.

For just one second she'd have liked to be back there again. In the Bookworm. In San Francisco. Just to see what it all looked like nowadays. Not because she thought Marek could ever love her again. No, just to observe. The way a fly on the wall would. Unnoticed.

A crazy idea, that one, she chided herself. Down there, far below, was Iran. Or Turkey, unless it was now

Ukraine they were crossing. Someplace. On the opposite side of the world from Marek Sumner.

As always.

Chapter Three

On the way to Carl's car, they passed the apartment Marek had once called home. The building hadn't really changed. Up there, on the second floor, panes of glass in the wide sash windows caught the flash of a late afternoon sun, turning them a glancing blue. Up there, he'd spent his time writing, stuffing his head with knowledge while the world had whirled on around him.

It had also been there, right in there, on just such a late afternoon, that Felicity Powers had first knocked on his door.

Marek passed a hand over his face as if trying to remove the cobwebs of time, perhaps make time disappear altogether. All these years had passed, and here he was, still nursing a memory. Stupid idea, going over all this old territory again! The ghost of his youth.

Damn this writer's memory that keeps all the images fresh, filled with their original poignancy. Fleeting, fairy tale images, he chided himself. Nothing to do with reality. The past always takes on a mysterious dreamlike quality.

Most likely, if Felicity Powers crossed his path these days, she wouldn't seem so exceptional. She'd be like all the other women he'd made love to, known briefly, then untangled himself from. She'd had such an impact upon him back then because he'd been young, naïve, relatively inexperienced. Rendering too important the first moment when Felicity had marched, quite deliberately, into his world.

That, he could remember in detail, as if it had happened only minutes ago.

He'd been up there, in the apartment, trying to work, writing that paper of his: the role of women in Thomas Hardy's novels and Hardy's notion of sensuality and subsequent punishment. Six o'clock in the evening, and out in the street the sun was still shining. He had to do his utmost to concentrate, try to work above the hum of strumming guitars, the shouts of children, the audible pulse of life in the Haight in 1971. When he'd heard the knock on the door, he'd groaned with exasperation. There was nothing he liked less than being interrupted. Flinging his pencil on the table, he'd risen to answer.

At first, he'd been so surprised, he'd done nothing more but stand there and stare. He'd never expected see that mysterious woman again, the one who'd spoken to him in the Bookworm. Yet here she was. At his door. Her glittering brown eyes meeting his own. And sensing, perhaps, his indecision, his shock. He felt his throat go dry.

For how long—a minute, perhaps only a few seconds—did they stand there, examining each other?

Confusion had paralyzed him. Not her, evidently. She only waited, maintaining her gaze. Nothing suggested she might be the victim of the same inner turmoil consuming him. No, she looked confident, arch, knowing. As if she had a secret. As if she knew perfectly well nothing would ever be the same again.

Because it wouldn't. Something passionately strong and splendid stretched between them. Again.

Just like it had at their first meeting.

Finally, scraping his addled wits together, he'd stepped aside.

"Come in." The banal words sounded so silly. In front of her, all his habitual easy assurance had melted away. He'd become a foolish adolescent.

Or perhaps it was because the desire he felt for her was so tangible. Raw desire.

She swept in—no other way of putting it. Stopped when she was in the middle of the room. Turned slowly, her gaze taking in shelves sagging under the heavy weight of books, the desk with its seemingly disorganized mass of papers, the other books and heaped documents, one on top of the other, over every available surface.

Was her gaze still mocking or was it admiring as it skimmed over the framed Paul Klee prints on the white walls? A very threadbare fake oriental carpet covered the wooden planks on the floor; an ancient red plush sofa from the 1930s with scrolled wooden arms threw out a comforting welcome.

She didn't even bother hiding her bold curiosity, or that she was observing, noting, judging. Well, let her judge him if she wanted. He didn't have to justify himself, his life, his taste.

"A simple student's apartment, as you see," said Marek, dryly, breaking the silence.

Her smile was amused as she turned to him, her gaze unwavering. "At least there's nothing horrible."

"Horrible?" He arched an eyebrow, attempting to meet her condescension with a sneer of his own. "Such as a corpse under the desk? A blood-stained hatchet? You must be disappointed."

She laughed. It changed her entire face, transforming the almost severe, hawk-like features into something warmer, something infinitely touching. Her teeth were white, perfect; her smile was broad. Her head tilted back slightly on a long, elegant neck.

He was intensely aware that his fingers ached to reach out and touch her, pull her toward him, press her body against his, but he didn't dare. Indeed, he hardly trusted himself to move, lest she vanish.

"I should have said vulgar," she corrected, still grinning. "That's even worse."

"A blood-stained hatchet sounds good?"

"Wait!" She held up one hand in delighted protest. "This has nothing to do with blood and hatchets and corpses. And the word tacky is even better than vulgar."

"Tacky. I see. More or less..."

"You know. Posters of bare feet glued onto the ceiling, drinking glasses with nude women, or ceramic cups that look like breasts."

"I strike you as the kind of person who'd own stuff like that?" He forced himself to look offended.

"Looks can be deceiving. They usually are."

What image did she have of him? "How about a deck of pornographic playing cards with bare-assed men wearing short black socks and shiny shoes? Is that tacky enough for you?"

"Right! That really *is* one hundred percent tacky." She stopped, looked at him. "Don't tell me you've got those!"

"Okay. I won't."

"No. Wait. I didn't mean what I said. If you do have dirty playing cards, I want to know."

Why did she want to know? "Tell me first if tacky

is positive or negative."

"Are you joking? I just want to see you implicate yourself before things get going."

"Before what things get going?" A wild desire to laugh bubbled up inside of him.

For the first time she seemed to lose a little bit of her bright assurance. Something flickered in her eyes. Her expression changed again.

"Mind if I take a seat?"

She was sounding flippant in an effort to cover her confusion, Marek realized. *She's probably far more vulnerable then she lets on. This bravado, this cool confidence, it's all just a show. A very good show, indeed.* He watched her move toward the sofa, drop onto it casually, her thin, India print skirt flowing out around her. Yes, she was a sensitive, vibrant, easily-touched woman. And that made her more desirable than ever.

Then, suddenly, he knew it wasn't a simple question of desire. It was more. He felt his pulse quicken. *Slowly, slowly, Marek*, he told himself. *Don't ruin this.*

He smiled. "All right, I'll come clean. I don't have dirty playing cards. But I know someone who does: my father." He kept his face poker straight.

"Your father likes things like that?" Her nose wrinkled.

"You should see his bathing beauty drinking glasses. You add ice cubes, the glass gets frosty, and the bathing suits become transparent."

"Cute. Do you get to inherit those one day?"

"If they're the only things I inherit, I can cope."

"You like your father's taste, huh?"

"The man's a paragon in pretty well every field." His light tone couldn't disguise an edge of bitterness.

"What does this paragon do for a living?"

She was evidently the persistent sort. She didn't seem to care if her questions were in good taste or not. Why did she want to know about his father? Trying to check out if he was of a socially acceptable level? He wasn't. So why not answer her? Conversation was easing up the tension.

"My father passes the time drinking beer and watching television," Marek said blandly.

He sat down on the chair by his desk. There was room enough on the gigantic sofa for both of them, of course, but from this position he could observe her more efficiently. She wore a white, Indian cotton blouse that outlined the gentle sweep of her breasts. Her legs, visible at the hem of her skirt were slender, her ankles very fine, her feet long and bony in their espadrilles. His yearning stunned him because he knew it was still mixed with something else, something as yet nameless.

She's beautiful, absolutely beautiful, he mused, and the thought warmed him through and through.

"Where's your lady friend?" Her voice was unrelenting, and she'd raised one eyebrow with a certain arrogance. Once again, Marek had the feeling the bravado was definitely an act, a simple veneer she used to give herself courage.

"Myra. You mean Myra," he answered calmly.

"All right. Myra. Is she out rounding up the bean sprouts?"

The note of jealousy tickled him. "Are you always catty toward other women? It's sort of out of fashion these days."

"No," she answered without the slightest hesitation. "I'm never catty about other women. Just about Myra."

"You know Myra well?" Strange. He hadn't been aware the two women were acquainted. In fact, the other day in Bookworm, he could have sworn they didn't know each other at all. Myra had made a point of blatantly ignoring her.

"No, I don't know Myra well. In fact, I don't know Myra at all."

"I see." His lips twitched with a desire to smile. "This is about as clear as mud. You don't like Myra, but you don't know her."

Her eyes continued to meet his, their expression stony. Perhaps she was a nut? He hoped not. More than anything he wanted her not to be a nut.

"Look, how about if we start at the beginning." His voice was gentle. "For example, do you have a name? First name, last name, like almost everyone else around?"

She relaxed. "Felicity. Felicity Powers."

"Interesting contrast, that, Felicity and Powers. It does have me wondering if the name creates the person." He was relieved to see her lips curve into a smile again. "And what do you do in life, Felicity Powers?"

"Is this what you really want to know?" There was no mistaking her mockery now. "I mean, wouldn't you rather know why I'm catty about Myra?" She pronounced it My-rah, haughtily, nastily.

"All right. Why are you being catty about Myra? Did she poison your pet piranha recently? Myra's great, but I just can't keep her away from the strychnine."

"You really want me to tell you?"

"You really want to tell me, evidently."

"Because I'm here to seduce you. I want you." Her eyes, as they met his, were unwavering.

"I see." He blinked with surprise, stared, then wondered if he were in for a big disappointment. She was a nut after all.

She was waiting for him to react. Perhaps this was the time to ask her to leave? He couldn't. Instead, he noted how she suddenly bit her lip. As if she'd been caught out, playing this role she wasn't entirely comfortable with. He found himself grinning. "I must admit, of all the answers I expected, that wasn't one of them."

"And your response?" Her smile challenged.

"Hold on." He raised his hands. "What's the rush, Felicity Powers?" He liked the sound of the strange name on his tongue. Was it her real name or had she invented it to go along with this bravado she was displaying? "How about if we take this slowly. Like, first of all, I want to know why."

"Why what?" Uncertainty flashed in the brown eyes.

"Look." He shifted on his chair and tried not to burst out laughing. The situation was beginning to strike him as being very funny. If only she wasn't so intense. "Why do you want to seduce me?"

"Why?" She was surprised. She hesitated for a minute, as if this were the first time she'd ever thought about her intended seduction. Then, she shook her head. "Because you excite me. Because—" She stopped shrugged, looked away. "It's so simple, really. Because I find you beautiful, and I want to touch you." She faced him and changed key again. Her voice was cold and defensive now. "You aren't going to tell me a woman's never said that to you before, are you?"

"No. I'm not."

"You see?" The answer hadn't pleased her. Still, she braved it out. "Therefore it's a perfectly reasonable thing to say."

"As if pure desire is something perfectly reasonable," he said, his voice dry. "Which it isn't."

She looked at him blankly.

He took a deep breath. "Listen, Felicity Powers. I don't want to sound like a reluctant virgin here, but…um…I really would like to get to know you a little better first."

"What's the matter? Are you uncomfortable with what I said? Or are you just the usual, run-of-the-mill male chauvinist pig who always has to make the first move?"

"Because if I jump on you, tear off your clothes, plunge in, so to speak, that would convince you I'm not a male chauvinist pig?"

"Okay." Her lips curved upward devilishly. "Point taken."

"But the war's not won." He grinned back.

Her smile vanished; her eyes narrowed knowingly. "Or perhaps you're just one of those men who's incapable of functioning when a woman is so up front?"

Incapable of functioning? He felt like standing up, crossing the room and giving her a lusty demonstration of exactly how well he could function. He couldn't say the idea didn't excite him. And Felicity Powers was asking for it. Male chauvinist pig! Incapable of functioning like a man! This woman was too much.

"Obviously you've never handled anyone with kid gloves in your entire life," he chided. "You think you can say exactly what you want, and to hell with everyone else's feelings."

"So I was right! Or perhaps this is a new experience for you after all—"

"Actually, Felicity, women often come knocking on my door in order to seduce me. The difference is, they go into action as soon as they enter the room. They don't throw words and challenges at me. Making love isn't a challenge. At least, not for me it isn't."

She nodded, didn't seem in the least offended. Suddenly, in one swift and smooth movement she stood up, crossed to where he was sitting, and crouched at his feet. Her long fingers slid slowly between the inside of his thighs, moved upward. He was caught in the scent of her, a perfectly natural fragrance of flowers and incense, musk and fresh hay.

Close up like this he saw the beautiful perfection of her pale skin, the freckles covering every inch of her face. His eyes skimmed her finely etched mouth, and he almost moaned with the need to cover it with his own. A need he was about to refuse himself.

Swiftly, he trapped her two fine, long-fingered hands in one of his before she could go higher, before she could turn the tight hot flame burning in his groin into a raging storm. With his free hand he reached out, touched her cheek, caressed it softly.

He wanted her, all right. She wanted him. Desire stretched between them, palpable, hot.

"I meant what I said," he said softly, his voice husky. "You are absolutely beautiful, Felicity Powers. And sexy as hell. And exciting. I wouldn't be so stupid as to lie. I do want you, all right. I want you stretched out under me on my bed. I want to feel you, taste you, lick you. Everywhere."

As soon as he voiced the words, he knew how badly he wanted to do just that. Had he ever felt this strongly before? Had he ever desired anyone as much as he did this woman here at his feet? Heat coiled low in his belly, made him ache with need, and still he resisted.

She waited, her eyes fearful at first, then softening. "But?"

"As I said, I want to get to know you better. It's important for me, and I want it to be important for you too. And we have time, plenty of time, to do just that."

He forced himself to stand, pulled her up beside him. He longed to put his arms around her, feel the long, slender length of her, but he didn't dare. They'd never get out of this apartment if he did. Instead, he turned toward the door.

"Come." He reached out for her hand.

"Come where? Where are we going?" She held back warily. Evidently she felt as though her considerable powers of seduction had failed her.

He smiled down at her. "I'm going to buy you ice cream."

"Ice cream?" She said the words slowly, shaking her head slightly. Astonished.

"That's right," he said as if the proposal had been a perfectly normal one in perfectly normal circumstances. "Homemade ice cream. Don't you eat ice cream?"

"Of course I do."

"And then we're going for a nice walk."

"A nice walk?" Amusement tickled her eyes.

"Your words seem to echo my own." He smiled back at her, and suddenly the realization hit him: he was living one of those absolutely perfect moments that come so rarely in everyday life. Magic moments that sneak in surreptitiously, a blessed gift. That vanish at the slightest reproach.

****

The walk that evening was the very first of their long walks. Remembering the time, so long ago now, it seemed as if their two years together had been spent walking. Up Market, down Geary, down into the less savory areas off Mission where abandoned warehouses spewed rubbish from destroyed doors. There was no place in the city they didn't go. Out to the dreary, white-washed suburbs, out to the sea. Neither of them had money, neither had much patience for socializing. They avoided the cinema, only rarely visited other people's houses.

One thing was clear to Marek: from the moment Felicity Powers had entered his life, everything changed. It was as if he and Felicity needed silence, needed the intensity they found when cut off from everything and everyone around them. Or perhaps the isolation had created the intensity? No, certainly not. It had been intense from that first evening, from that very first walk to buy ice cream.

"Why are you feeling such a mad urge for ice cream?" Her voice was edged with curiosity, perhaps with a touch of resentment, as well.

"Not just any ice cream. Homemade ice cream." He looked down at her. "Felicity, do you always question everything?"

"Yes."

"I was afraid of that." He grimaced, sighed. "Okay. Ice cream seems nice and normal and I'm in the mood for nice normality. Can you accept something so simple?" Not that anything seemed either normal or simple. His head was spinning; his feet tripped across clouds.

In a way, the situation was funny, really it was. This beautiful woman, a woman he was very attracted to, had come to seduce him, and he'd refused her. Well, not exactly refused. Simply hesitated. He must be the crazy one! Any other male in the area would have pulled Felicity over to the bed, spent the next few hours having a very erotic experience and then gone out for ice cream—if the two of them found they had enough in common to warrant such an act. But not Marek. He always did things the wrong way around.

He glanced at Felicity. She must find him ridiculous. She felt his eyes on her, turned, met his gaze evenly. And smiled. No, she didn't think him ridiculous. She didn't.

She walked with a long, loose, almost gawky, swinging stride as if she covered miles like this every day. Her head with its riotous flame of hair was held high, her shoulders back. Marek felt suddenly proud to be walking with her, to be seen with her. It wasn't as if he wasn't proud to be with Myra. It was simply…it felt right being here, beside this straight-standing, rangy woman. Their steps matched, their pace, their demeanor. There was a feeling of symmetry, of perfection.

"Vanilla and chocolate? Here at Marty's you have the choice of fifteen different and very exotic ice creams, and you choose vanilla and chocolate?"

"It's all I like." Her expression was defiant, stubborn.

"And you're ready to defend your position with your life, I see." He was amused. "Do you always rise to battle like this over banalities?"

"A choice of ice cream certainly isn't a banality." She took the cone in her hand and Marek noticed the length of her fingers, the fineness of her bones. Her wrist was very slender, almost thin. She angled her face up at him, and the golden, evening sun caught her cheekbones. "For the next ten minutes I'm going to have the pleasure of eating the best ice cream in town. I'll be damned if I accept someone else's opinion as to what's good and what isn't." She licked at her cone with a sharp, pink cat's tongue, closed her eyes and sighed. "Wonderful."

"As I promised."

They began to walk, leaving the main street for the quiet back ones, losing track of where they went. He tried to stop his heart from pounding so wildly, his head from spinning. Then gave up the attempt altogether.

"You like going for walks?"

"Sure. Why not?" She looked at him strangely. Perhaps she wasn't the sort of woman who indulged in much normal, banal conversation. "My feet are so huge I reckon I was meant to cover miles." She grinned with a certain embarrassment.

"Huge?" He looked down. "Long feet, true. Not huge. Elegant, perhaps."

"Not glass slipper material, in any case."

"Miserable things for walking, glass shoes."

They walked until sky had darkened and the street lamps had clicked on. When they reached the Haight again, they found a bench not far away from a scrubby little park, and sat down.

He'd found out she was a drama student at the university, that she lived on a small allowance from her family, and she shared a Victorian house with three other people.

"It's anything but a cozy arrangement," she'd said. "When you live with people, all the worst in you seems to come out. It's all very well to say you love every human being on the surface of the earth, but it just isn't true. In a very short time, you begin to hate the smell of their cooking, their taste in music, the way they cough. Just hearing them move across the room right above your head, and your skin starts to prickle."

"That's a rather radical point of view."

"Obviously. Especially in this day and age in the Haight, when you're supposed to be cool, really cool. Don't you ever get the feeling you've been dropped into a society where a sort of group lobotomy has taken place? I mean, everyone has these fatuous smiles on their faces most of the time. And then they tell you all the right answers are in Mao's little red book. And then everyone says, 'Yeah. Right on.' And that's supposed to be a discussion."

"Then why don't you get out of the area?"

"Get out? Don't get me wrong. It's better here than out there. Out there, men dressed up in green pajamas get sent over to another part of the world where they have to kill off men in black pajamas."

"So if you disagree with everything, what are you going to do about it?"

"Run away."

"Where are you running? It's bad in here, and bad

out there. What's the choice?"

"Europe perhaps. India maybe. It's a big world, Marek. I have to get out there and see for myself."

"What about your studies?"

"What studies? I'm majoring in theater, and I see how banal it is, how nasty and backbiting all the amateur performers are. I mean, we are supposed to be *studying*, for heaven's sake. Not hating the person who gets a leading role in the college play."

"I guess that's a foretaste of the real theater world."

"What a world!" Felicity rolled her eyes.

"So study something else."

"I am. I'm taking a minor in history and it's wonderful when—and if—you get a professor who's fascinating. They exist. Really they do. But there are also the dull pedants." She sighed. "I think I've worked out university isn't for me. I want to do things. See with my own eyes, not sit in a classroom and absorb."

He was amused by her intensity. Well, it was amusing if you decided not to fight her every single step of the way. Otherwise, it would be rough going. Her eyes flashed. She sat straight in her seat as if ready for action at any minute. When she spoke, her hands gestured wildly. Vibrant! A vibrant woman. No other word could describe her so adequately.

"But you're working toward a degree?"

"Degrees!" She sat back, flicked her hand airily as if the very word could only be met with contempt. "I've decided to refuse marks and degrees. I made the choice to audit all of my courses. Then, when I learn, it's for the pleasure of acquiring knowledge only. Not for any rotten piece of paper enabling me to succeed one day in a conformist world." This last was a sneering, mocking declaration. And a challenge.

Silently they watched people filter past them, most of them young, the men bearded, the women in long skirts, everyone longhaired. The atmosphere was relaxed, but the night had turned cool. He looked at her, saw she seemed lost in her thoughts, off somewhere else. Then, he felt her shiver. She must be freezing in her skimpy blouse and thin skirt, thought Marek suddenly.

He knew he wanted her to stay. She was a burning comet searing into his atmosphere and he wanted—needed—to bask in the violent light she exuded.

He reached out for her, pulled her tightly into his warmth. Softly, passively she folded herself against him, lowered her head onto his shoulder, and the gesture reached deep inside of him. So *Passionata*, this woman of fire, could also be tender, gentle.

"You're cold."

"No." Her voice was muted, subdued. "It's too exciting just being beside you to feel cold."

The words dug into his gut.

"Come on." He pulled her to her feet and they began to walk again, back across the park, back through the night streets. Cars roared past, people milled around them. There was music, clamor. There were bright lights and a waft of incense. He didn't notice any of it. Only this counted. This walk. This woman he held. This tension, this hot, liquid flow of energy.

He didn't bother to turn on the lights in the apartment. The room was lit from the lamps out in the street and he could see her perfectly, the arch of her brows, the delicate frame. Slowly he undid the buttons of her blouse. She wore no brassiere, and her skin was hot, burning to his touch as he cupped her full, soft breasts in his hands.

Moaning, she pushed herself more tightly against him, arched her hips against his groin.

How did they manage to get out of the rest of their clothes? All those buttons and zippers seemed impossible obstacles to their trembling fingers. Eventually they stood naked in the middle of the room, not touching now, caressing only with their eyes.

She was very slender, almost bony and exceedingly delicate. Holding his eyes with her own, she reached up, loosened the clips that held her hair in place and slowly the thick, splendid mass tumbled down, over her shoulders, down her back. Then she waited, watching him.

Somehow they found the bed. As if in a dream he saw her, silhouetted against the white sheets, stretched out, arching, reaching for him. He gasped as their bodies met and reality vanished. They tasted, stroked, slowly, passionately. He'd never known a woman so generous, so touching, so filled with desire for him. She licked his skin, tasting him, exploring, making him wild with yearning. When he finally entered her, filling her hot tightness, the pleasure made his mind reel as never before.

It was as if he understood what the word passion meant for the first time in his life. As if he'd finally found out why sex could be called "making love."

"I love you," she'd said.

Raising himself onto one elbow, he'd looked down into her face, pale in the night. Her eyes were dark, deep, and the emotion he saw etched into every single one of her features told him exactly what he wanted to know. She loved him. It was true. She loved him, Marek Sumner. She loved him because two people could never be closer. She loved him because they were meant for each other.

"And I love you," he'd answered softly. It was true. He loved this woman who, only a few hours ago, had been nothing more than a memory, a fleeting image caught in a bookstore.

It was a love that would last in time. He'd known that also.

Chapter Four

Felicity stood blinking in the bright light. Traffic roared around her and hot exhaust fumes shook the fronds of dusty palms with their feet set into the cement sidewalk. Well, here she was. In San Francisco. Suffering from culture shock, travel fatigue, jet lag, and the bizarre feeling of having fallen into a time warp.

Strange, being back here.

San Francisco! It was a city just like any other, when you came right down to it. A big city with roller coaster hills, and wooden houses, and main streets, and parks, and mild weather. There was nothing to hate, nothing to fret about. It was even more picturesque than many places. Of course, it had changed considerably over the years, but so had everywhere else in the world—including the South Pole.

Then why had she disliked this city so much back then? Why had she been so angry? Why had she fought so hard to get out? Why had she thought this was the worst place on earth? It was hard to find the answers to those old questions; so much time had passed, and she'd changed so much. Or had she? Well, that's what she was here for. To find out. And to confront her past.

No, she wasn't, she chided herself. Why kid herself. She was here because she wanted to see Marek again—and if that wasn't a crazy, hare-brained scheme, she didn't know what was! Running after a man she hadn't seen, spoken to, or even written to, since the nineteen-seventies. Cruising for a bruising.

You saw what he looked like in the newspaper photo, the photo you still have tucked into your bag. Gorgeous, he looked. Sexy. Wonderful, just like he always did.

And you, Felicity Powers? I mean, just take a look at yourself. You look like you've been traveling for almost a whole week—which, in fact, you have. Raggedy clothes, worn down shoes, pale and exhausted-looking skin, white hair, wrinkles.

Anything else?

Not exactly the way you want to be looking when you're about to confront a dream.

She sighed. She had a choice: get moving. Or just continue to stand here, running herself down, rolling out the flaws. If she did, she'd demolish every last bit of courage she'd managed to scrape together. And then she'd have to turn right around, jump into the first taxi rolling past, and demand to be driven back to the airport, pronto!

There was no reason for her to feel so nervous, was there? She'd lived a magical life full of adventure, full of danger. She'd done exactly what she'd wanted to do. Even if she looked nothing like the young woman she'd been back then, at least she could hold up her end of the conversation!

Her hands were icy cold. Why was her heart beating so wildly? Why was she here on the sidewalk, out in this sun-doused evening, hesitating? Hardly daring to cross the road? Searching for the courage she needed to keep on walking? She took a deep breath, hoisted the red strap of her heavy blue bag onto her shoulder and stepped off the curb.

Stopped. Stared. After spending all those years in the world's hidden niches, she'd forgotten if you turned left or right on Haight to get to the Bookworm.

****

Carl had predicted a fair-sized crowd would show up for the book signing, but he'd under-estimated Marek's pulling power. If any more people managed to crowd in here, the walls of the Bookworm would pop apart at the corners.

Marek's hand had been shaken at least a thousand times, and he'd managed to find the right words to greet long lost and often long forgotten "friends." And now, at this very moment, he was so weary, all his polite words were sticking in his throat. He stared down at the person standing in front of him, and hoped he'd successfully managed to hide his embarrassed wonder.

Almost forty-three years! Only forty-three years since they'd been intimate? It seemed like a hundred and forty-three, a thousand, or even a million. Would he even have been able to pick her out in a crowd? Would he have recognized her in this room if she hadn't come up to him in this way? No, probably not.

She was attractive still. Not lovely like she had been. The long, straight golden hair falling like a thick, shining curtain down her back was now cropped short into an elegant, practical style, one suitable for a chic woman in her sixties. Still slender, she had, nonetheless, adopted a maternal attitude that aged her. There was a certain tense watchfulness in her eyes, a defiant tightness to her mouth. As if Myra defied him to criticize the individual she'd become.

As if he would, he thought. Everyone did the best

they could. The life Myra had chosen had, most probably, suited her perfectly.

"Marek, meet my husband, Sam. Sam Parsons."

He found himself shaking the hand of a tall, evidently prosperous person.

"A pleasure to meet you," said Sam with a warm smile. "Especially after all Myra's told me about you."

What, exactly, would she have said, Marek wondered. How did a person talk about an ex-lover? Did Sam Parsons even know what his relationship with Myra had once been?

"Things certainly have changed since the sixties, haven't they? Not that I was involved in the hippie scene myself," Sam said, smiling still. "I was a deadly serious law student in Texas. For me, San Francisco was at the other end of the world."

The crowd around them had become even denser. Clearly several people were waiting patiently for Marek to give them his attention.

"We have so much to catch up on, Marek!" Myra's smile was still tense, painfully tight.

Do we? Marek looked down at Myra. What did they really have to say to each other? Even all those long years ago, they'd been so different. What was there to catch up on now?

"No doubt." It was a coward's way out, and he knew it. He'd no reason to hurt Myra's feelings—not again!

"You'll come and have dinner with us, of course. How long are you staying?"

"I only have a few days in California, and I'm planning to head down the coast. There probably won't be much chance to get together this time. But I'll be back." He shot them what was supposed to be a conclusive smile. The idea of dinner with Myra and Sam didn't sound like something he'd ever want to do.

In actual fact, he was as free as a bird. The trip down the coast was a desperate, spur of the moment plea. As free as a bird? Did those high flying creatures have hearts weighing in at half a ton? His eyes flickered over the crowd. No doubt he'd once known quite a few of these people, but he couldn't recognize them now. Why on earth had he thought this sentimental journey would be enjoyable? At the moment, it was about as full of laughs as a funeral.

If only Felicity...Impossible! One unusually hot day, when a shimmering sun had turned sidewalks into blazing cement squares, melted black tar streets into shoe-clutching ooze, Felicity had boarded a charter plane. Brussels, then London. London, Glasgow. Glasgow, Paris. The world was such a big place after all—you never realized just how big until you wanted to find someone again.

"Tomorrow," Myra was saying. "You can make it tomorrow, can't you? For dinner. You'll still be around tomorrow." It wasn't a question. It contained just a faint, but still discernible, edge of aggression.

"Tell me where you're staying," said Sam. "I can come and pick you up. It's not far. We live in Forest Hills."

No, there was no way he could wiggle his way out of this. Might as well look gracious even though he felt like a condemned man in front of the firing squad. "Please don't bother picking me up. I don't have the faintest idea where I'll be tomorrow. It'll be just as easy for me to hop into a cab."

"If you're sure? I get home from the office at around seven, so if you come a little early, you and Myra can hash over the old memories." He chuckled. "Knowing Myra, you'll also get a full tour of the house and garden plus a half hour session with the family photo album."

"Sam!" Myra threw a slightly pained look up at her spouse. "I wouldn't want to bore Marek with such dull, domestic trivia."

Still, Marek noted, she didn't look as though the program distressed her. He could see the evening stretching out in front of him: a stroll through the suburbs of Hell minus the dash and glory of fire and brimstone. Conventional, uninspiring. He'd be expected to find suitable praise for the decor, the house, the garden, the offspring and the offspring's offspring—if there were any of those. He knew the score. He'd been through hundreds of such evenings in his life. He could survive another one. He felt he owed it to Myra, somehow. To acknowledge her domestic success.

That resolved, it was now back to shaking hands and smiling. How long would this go on? Hours? It was feeling like centuries. He knew there were more people, over there on the left.

****

He didn't look in her direction, not even once, Felicity saw. If he'd looked up, he probably wouldn't even have noticed her anyway, half-hidden, as she was, behind the bookshelves. *Fading into the scenery*, she sneered at herself.

All his attention was directed toward the people he spoke with. He'd always managed to do that: give his all to whomever he was with at the moment, as if what they had to say was of utmost importance. He was really classy looking. Elegant in that sports jacket, in those dark gray, beautifully cut trousers. His glasses underlined the intelligence in his face. Even over this distance, the influence he was having on her was astounding—and it had nothing to do with the past. Admit it! Didn't she now have the answer to the question that had been plaguing her for so long?

Would he still have the same effect on you now that he had before?

Yes!

She felt as if she'd been thrust into a dangerous, highly volatile, situation. *Cool down, Felicity. He has a wife here somewhere.*

Fine laugh lines crinkled around the green of his eyes. His mouth was resolute, impatient. A curl of salt and pepper hair had tumbled over his forehead, and she'd have given just about anything in the world to have the courage to go over, touch it, brush it back. *You don't have the right to do that anymore! You gave up that right a long time ago.*

Still, the thought didn't stop the tingle in her fingers, the desire to reach out. He had aged. Of course he had. But he'd done it wonderfully. He glowed. Whereas she was looking like she'd just managed to crawl out of the swamp. She'd better get out of here. And fast. Before anyone noticed her, weak coward that she was. Besides, wasn't it better to leave a dream intact? The dream of the wonderful things that would happen if she and Marek came face to face again after all this time. That was only a dream. A real encounter would destroy everything, all the illusions. Is that what she wanted? Of course not.

So what did she want? She knew now—now that she'd seen him again. She wanted to know he loved her. Still. She wanted him to desire her madly. She wanted to be with him, skin against skin, his beautiful mouth on hers, telling her it wasn't too late. That the intervening years had been as empty for him as they had been for her. Her heart thudded with the violence of her hopes. *Fool*!

She watched him as he stood near the table piled high with copies of his books, right at the center of an enthusiastic crowd. Who were all these people anyway? She must have known some of them once, but now she was unable to recognize anyone at all. Good, solid, middle-class Californians, that's what they all looked like. They must be the very same people she'd known here in the Haight back then. The rebels. The revolutionaries who were going to change the country, turn it inside out, create the greatest socialist democracy that had ever existed. She smiled to herself. The revolution of flowers had faded as quickly as a cut rose.

And her throat felt like the surface of the Sahara at midday. Was she going to make a run for it? Yes? No? Of course not. She couldn't.

There was a temporary lull around the table. Marek bent to sign a book.

Move! Felicity shoved herself out of her hiding place. If only her legs didn't feel as weak as wet noodles. How, in heaven's name, did you cross a room on noodles?

If only he didn't look so...so beautiful. Yes, that's what he was. Absolutely beautiful—but then, he always had been. Sexy as hell!

"Hi." *Brilliant starter, Felicity! That should*

impress him all right.

Hi? The hand on the page he was signing, stopped. He didn't move, didn't look up. Not immediately. What was going on? What was he thinking?

A few seconds passed—just a few seconds while reason fought with hope in her heart. She braced herself…

Then, so very slowly, he raised his eyes. "Felicity?"

Stunned surprise tugged at her heart. He'd recognized her voice. After all this time.

"I must be dreaming," he said softly. "This isn't possible." He straightened, shook his head in wonderment, stared at her as if she were a ghost. "But here you are. Felicity Powers."

She stared back more boldly now, searching his face just the same way he was searching hers. Looking for messages.

Then, he was moving. Was on her side of the table. Reaching out, pulling her into his embrace as if time had never intervened. She enlaced him, melted against him. Closing her eyes, she wished time could stop, leave her here forever. Here, where she belonged.

Holding tightly in a world containing only the two of them, the noise of the crowd receded, became a vague murmur, the sigh of a distant wind.

Until he finally managed to let her go. Stepping back, he looked slightly abashed.

"Your husband is going to have something to say about a hug like that." His voice was almost light, teasing. Almost. Had the word "husband" bothered him? She hoped so.

"No husband. I've been divorced for ages." What

did she see on his face? Surprise? Pleasure? She'd been right. He had minded. Then she told herself to cut out the dreaming. Swallowing, shaking her head slowly, she sank down in the depths of his green gaze. "Your wife will mind, though."

"No wife."

"But I read—" She stopped, stared up.

"Ex-wife." His smile was faint. "A long time ago, too."

He was divorced! Free! The news shook her, leaving her stunned. Instantly it was as if a bright light had snapped on allowing life to take on colors she'd never seen before.

Don't get carried away, she reprimanded herself. There must be a woman hanging around somewhere. Of course there must. Still, there was hope.

"That's good." She stopped abruptly, bright pink flooding into her cheeks. "Damn! What a terrible thing to say," she sputtered. "I mean, perhaps you're unhappy about it." She stopped. With every word she was padding even more deeply into a gluey morass.

He threw back his head in a peal of bright laughter, and relief flooded through her.

"I guess you're not." She began to laugh, too.

People had started watching them, reminding them they were in the midst of a crowd.

"What the hell are you doing here, Felicity Powers!"

She smiled up at him, her eyes expressing a faint confusion. "You don't mind?" What a crazy thing to say. Where had her brain skittered off to?

He was still looking amazed, as if unable to believe she really was here, standing in front of him. "Mind?"

he said slowly. "Why would I mind? I just never imagined a memory would ever become reality again."

"Neither did I." Her throat was so tight, she could hardly squeeze out the words. "It almost didn't. It'll sound crazy if I tell you how I got here." The warmth in his eyes made her ache. Part of her had forgotten intensity like this really did exist.

"Go on." His lips curved upward. As if it didn't matter what she said, what they talked about.

"I was in a plane, flying over Iran two days ago, and I was handed an *International Herald Tribune*. You were in it." It sounded crazy, extreme, nutty. Bad image. She didn't want him to think she was crazy, or strange, or someone to be avoided. He mustn't move away from her, dismiss her, reject her. "Look, I'm not making this up."

"Who said you were? Sounds banal, commonplace." He could still tease her. It still felt good.

She grinned, her heart leaping. "Doesn't it just. The article talked about San Francisco and the Bookworm."

He shrugged. "So you hijacked the plane and here you are."

"Why hijack? It's so much easier just to go buy a ticket. I was on my way to Frankfurt. I caught a flight from there to Paris, then Paris to New York, and another to San Francisco. And here I am." She gestured airily with her hands as if the trip had been little more trouble than a local bus ride.

"Here you are." His voice was so soft she hardy recognized it.

Here she was, all right. And now what? They were in the middle of a crowd, the middle of a room. He was the star, here. She couldn't drag him away or monopolize him.

"I only got in an hour ago. I got here as fast as I could. I didn't want to miss you." She smiled faintly. "That would have been ridiculous after coming so far."

It probably had been ridiculous to come here anyway. Ridiculous. They'd said hello. Now he would move off, talk to someone else, and she could just as well roar back out to the airport. An eight thousand mile detour for a hi.

"You could simply have telephoned." His eyes glinted with humor.

"I wanted to see you. I needed to." True confession time! She was laying it on too thick. She was sounding like a stalker, and any second now, he'd take to his heels.

Still, he must see how uncertain she felt. He hadn't stopped watching her. Why didn't he say something? She had only a limited time—a few seconds—before someone interrupted them. He couldn't deny the energy and excitement shimmering between them, could he?

Or was she the only one feeling it? Was he pulling back?

"What I'm about to say will convince you I'm crazy." She took an unsteady breath. "Up there in the clouds, I felt as if destiny had put the article in the paper on that very day. I mean, I hadn't been anywhere near a newspaper for months on end. And the one time I am…" She stopped, then grimaced, mocking herself, ridiculing this idea of hers. "I know how silly it sounds. Why the hell should destiny be interested in me?"

"Marek, there's a journalist waiting for you..." It was Carl, evidently flustered. He stopped suddenly, saw her. Did a double take. "I don't believe this. Is it you, Felicity?"

"Carl!" She reached out, hugged him briefly.

"You haven't changed! Or—well, not a lot, anyhow." Carl chuckled despite his nervousness. "Can you let me have Marek for a minute?"

"Of course," said Felicity, and forced herself to laugh brightly. He wasn't hers to give. Her time was up. She'd done her best. The next move was his.

Marek had to do something, say something. He had to! He had to feel the same way about this! He had to see how important it was. Felicity held her breath, watched him.

"Will you stay?" Marek looked at her, his eyes veiled now.

"Do you want me to?" Her heart was pounding painfully.

"Oh yes. I want you to. Don't disappear."

Her heart began pumping. He wasn't turning her down, wasn't pulling back. Maybe he could accept something might happen between the two of them? She had to be honest with him, perfectly honest. "I was hoping you wanted me to." She said it softly. "I didn't really come all this way just to disappear again."

He beamed down at her, the green eyes glinting with a reckless, encompassing wildness. "We have to be alone." It was a promise.

She nodded unable to speak. Pure, simple utter happiness coursed through her. Idiotic joy, brilliant hope.

He moved off.

Someone—it must have been Carl—pushed a drink into her hand. People came over to her. Conversation hummed around her, and she knew she must be participating. Still, she couldn't have told anyone what she was saying or even if she spoke at all.

All her thoughts were for Marek. Just being in the same room with him was fantastic. She was almost afraid to let herself believe this was happening. It was as if she were simply sitting somewhere and dreaming of him, just as she had all these long years. Only this time it wasn't a dream. The rainbow lining of fantasy had split open, was teasing her with hope.

She watched him as he moved, so effortlessly, through the crowd. Tall, compelling, his looks were based on bone structure mixed with just the right amount of grace and authority. He smiled to everyone, warmly, reassuringly. It didn't matter if he never looked her way. He knew she was here, and he wanted her to stay!

She watched as women approached him. It still was there, his charm, his pull. He made wives want to forget they had husbands. She saw how he bent his head and said something to a tall, tense-looking woman who nodded, threw him a grateful look. The heavy-set man beside her wasn't looking anywhere near so rapturous as she was.

"We'll be having dinner together when this is over. You'll join us, won't you?"

Felicity turned toward the voice. Carl again. His eyes were questioning, sympathetic.

"Of course. I'd love to." She looked at him with relief. How did he know? "Thank you for thinking of me."

He didn't answer, but the look he threw her had a certain wickedness. Had Marek said something? No, she was being foolish. What would Marek have said? Years had passed. So many years. Then she shook herself. *Stop getting your hopes up. Perhaps nothing will happen. What makes you think he wants more than friendship? You belong to the past. You are a brief love story from the old days.*

A story she had ended so abruptly.

Her heart ached when she thought of how she'd opposed him back then. But had he given her a choice?

****

She remembered standing by the window staring down into the street. Down there, on the steps, the street musicians strummed their guitars, pale copies of Dylan and Guthrie. The usual crowd milled about laughing, sitting on the concrete steps. Children screamed, raced up and down the road, their long hair flying.

Behind her, in the room, Marek was at his desk, working, writing.

"Everyone looks the same," she'd muttered. "Identical." Her voice had been hard, bitter.

Marek had only sighed, then fought to concentrate on what he was writing, to ignore her.

"You'd think—if anyone thinks around here—these people who rant and rave about being different would strive for a little originality, wouldn't you? But no. Here we all are. Carbon copies. Just like the straights we're all so busy criticizing."

Marek had put down his pen, closed his eyes, and leaned back in his chair. There was no way of stopping her when she was in a mood like this. She continued, inexorable.

"The only difference is everyone's traded in their suits and ties and crew cuts for jeans and beards, long hair and tie-dye. And instead of Frank Sinatra and Mantovani, it's the Mamas and the Papas, Deep Purple, and Rotary Connexion. Nobody questions anything. No one dares contradict. Mass taste, mass opinion." Her voice had taken on a jagged, scathing edge. "And to think this is supposed to be a revolution!"

"Felicity, we've been over all this before, you know." He'd rubbed his eyes with fatigue. "Many, many times."

"Oh yes," she had spit back resentfully. "I know. And now you want me to shut up. You have to work. You don't have time to talk. Right?"

"Right. I do have this paper to finish." His voice had been calm, slightly removed.

His calm, his patience, that steady character of his, had always made her feel like even more of a monster. Not that feeling like a monster ever stopped her. "Of course. Just stick your head in your books and hide, Marek. That's what's important."

"Look, can't you stop criticizing everything? Live your own life. It doesn't matter what the others believe or do. No one's talking anarchy out there. This is supposed to be the 'People's' revolution. That means a revolution of the mass, with mass taste, and mass ideas."

"How can anyone expect a revolutionary new world if people don't even know how to think for themselves?" Exasperation made her desperate.

He'd stood up, come over to her and pulled her into his arms. She was tight, tense, hostile, but it only lasted for a minute. He only needed to touch her, hold her like this, and her anger evaporated. She folded herself against him.

"Couldn't we get out of here? Can't we leave? The world is so big. Huge. Vast. There are things to see, to experience. Please, Marek, can't we leave this place?"

"Yes, yes, my beauty," he'd moaned softly. "We can leave. One day. Not now. I can't go now, you know that."

"I know, I know, I know. You have to do your thesis. Don't tell me again. I've heard those words at least a thousand times now." She'd pulled back, looked up at him, pleadingly. "But don't you see? I feel like my life is slipping through my fingers. I hate this forced immobility."

"You think it sounds stupid when I say it's only for a few years." His eyes had been hooded, cool, watchful. Sent out a warning.

Which she'd ignored. "Yes. It sounds stupid because I can see what will happen in the future. You'll finish your thesis. Then what? Then you'll find a teaching job in some rotten university in some ghastly university town. Then you'll start pressing for children. And you'll try to appease me, saying we can go away in the summer—when the children are old enough to travel, that is."

"You're so certain of that?" He'd wanted to oppose her, tell her she was wrong. But was she? Wasn't security and a loving family exactly what he needed, craved? Hoped for? Yes. He dreamed of having children with her wild red tangle of hair. Her temperament.

"I'm scared of being buried alive before I live," she'd whispered. "I shouldn't even be here with you, should I? I should run for my life now, I know it."

"But?"

"But I love you so much."

She'd held on more tightly, as if she could—somehow—avoid a separation that seemed inevitable.

"And I love you so much," he'd whispered into her warm, fragrant mass of fiery hair.

And they had separated. There had been nothing else they could do. He'd stayed on, to build his career. She'd left to discover the world, to find out what life was all about. And in all that time, she'd never forgotten him, never doubted that, somehow, they'd been meant for one another.

****

And now? She'd done what she'd set out to do in life. She'd had a mission—of sorts—and had carried it out to the best of her ability. Now she was back, back in his life and ready for him. She had to make him understand that. She had to make him see she'd come home. To him. Just in case he still wanted her. Just in case he might be able to love her again.

Crazy ideas.

Only a crazy woman would have dreams like that.

Chapter Five

Felicity Powers beside him again?

She'd crossed continents to see him. Now, here she was, sitting beside him at this dinner table. For what must have been the hundredth time this evening, his eyes slid over toward her. He needed to see her; he had to confirm the reality of her presence.

She was different now. Very different. Or was she? Still slender, fragile-looking. The mass of hair, wild, rebellious still, and just as long, was caught—with very little success—into a high knot. *Some things never change*. The fiery red color had faded entirely, was replaced by a chaos of white and silver. But the same luminous, dark eyes sparkled in a face intense with excitement. Here were the soaring cheekbones, the arched nose, and thin mocking mouth. Both the sun and time had etched lines into the skin around her eyes, her mouth, her forehead.

Her very presence was stirring deep old emotions inside of him, emotions so intense, he was almost loathe to acknowledge them.

Just now she sat, chin cupped in the palm of her hand, talking to a tedious, convinced-looking woman with short-cropped gray hair. Who was the woman? Her face was vaguely familiar. He scrabbled about in the back of his mind searching for a label. Harriet? No. Hatty? Something similar, but far stranger. Wait.

Heppia? Heppia! Heppia White.

And no, she wasn't talking to Felicity: she was monologuing at her, not giving her the choice of refusal.

"Bshwarma teaches us Einstein's theory of time was basically correct. You know? Like, when you travel faster than the speed of light, time goes in reverse. But as Bshwarma points out, the basic solution lies elsewhere."

Heppia White, ex-revolutionary. Maoist, if he remembered correctly. Radical, verbose, advocate of violence against what she'd called "this traditional system run by pigs." At the same time, Heppia had held down a full-time job as supervisor in the phone company. The contrast hadn't seemed to bother her one whit. How had she justified her participation in "the system" back then? Marek remembered perfectly.

"Revolution has to come from the inside. We need infiltrators. That's where I come into the picture."

Well, the picture had altered with time—or was it the frame that had changed? Heppia White, forty-odd years along, had switched allegiances. Clearly, she'd become the member of some bizarre sect. Dressed in a long flowing robe of a strange, nauseating green, she resembled nothing more than a popped dirigible with a large, nodding head. A complicated silver medallion on a heavy chain swayed back and forth, emphasizing her words.

"So you see—" Heppia's electric drill voice pierced on inexorably. "Bshwarma says we can experience consecutive time, where things have neither a beginning nor an end. When you're enlightened enough, your life pattern starts to make sense." She stopped. Bent closer to Felicity with a look of complicity. "If you understand what I mean."

Felicity nodded obediently, but now Marek thought he could detect the old cynical sparkle in her eyes. "Oh, I do understand. Really and truly, I do. Like, uh, you can drink your cup of tea before pouring it out?"

"Marek! Where did you get your inspiration for *Heading Down*? Is Peirson based on a real person?" Leyland Rucker leaned across the table, his beefsteak face shiny with enthusiasm.

Marek dragged his eyes away from Felicity once more, dutifully rejoined the conversation. "Absolutely. Plenty of Joseph McCarthy's victims are still alive today."

But he had no wish to elaborate. It was high time to call this part of the evening to an end. He could tell Felicity was fighting to keep her eyes open—hadn't she said she'd been traveling for days? Yes. It was obvious, too. Her face was pale, almost translucent, and there were deep blue circles under her slanting, brown eyes. In fact, she resembled nothing so much as a delicate hot-house plant some uncaring brute had shoved out into a cold winter night. A sharp shard of guilt pierced Marek's consciousness.

Here she was, thrust into his world. He had the definite feeling this now-unknown Felicity Powers wasn't used to such social dinners. Not anymore. What exactly was she used to? He knew nothing about her, Marek realized. Nothing about the person she was, or about the life she'd lived. She'd mentioned being an aid worker, but, to him, that was an unknown quantity. Come to think of it, perhaps the exotic plant image wasn't far off the mark. At least one thing was certain:

he wouldn't get any information about this Felicity while he sat here, at this long table, in the over-heated room, discussing the merits of contemporary American writers or rehashing the "words of truth" issued by fashionable West Coast Gurus.

Surreptitiously, he glanced down at his watch. So late? Good! Surely he could make a break for it now without offending anyone.

And when you do get her out of here, when you leave with her on your arm, then what?

Exactly! What *did* he want? What was he going to do with her?

And what about Felicity? What were her plans? Did she have any? Would she want to go with him? Did she have anywhere to go? All her belongings seemed to be in that cheap blue nylon bag they'd dragged from the Bookworm to Carl's house. There it was now, waiting patiently in a corner by the door.

Was he just going to invite her back to his hotel room, just like that? Of course he wasn't. You couldn't do things like that—even though the very thought was mighty tempting. Life's landscape was starting to look exceedingly complicated.

"Tired?" Marek asked her softly. He saw relief in her eyes.

"Exhausted." She nodded. "Why deny it? I've pinched my arm so often in the last two hours in desperate attempts to stay awake, it's almost black and blue. I guess I shouldn't have had all this wine. Lovely wine. But on top of jet lag, I mean. Perhaps it just wasn't the right thing to do…"

"Then why don't we get out of here?"

"I don't want you to think I'm a party-pooper.

Besides, this is your big evening, right?"

He nodded slowly. "Oh yes. This is my big evening, all right."

He saw her swallow, saw her eyes soften, and he felt his own pulse quicken. Felt bright, glittery anticipation sneak back into the picture.

"What time is it now?" she asked.

"One fifteen."

"Really?"

"Why would I lie?"

"I suppose, what I mean is, it feels more like four fifteen." She stopped, slightly embarrassed. He saw the heat rising to her cheeks. "Sorry. I don't know if I really should have admitted that. It sounds so ungrateful." She tried to force a bright smile. "The food has been lovely. And everyone's so nice."

"And boring." He chuckled, keeping his voice low.

She exploded into relieved laughter.

"Tell me, when was the last time you slept?"

"Tomorrow or days ago. Who knows? My notion of time has turned into silly putty." She started giggling wildly as pure exhaustion threatened her control. "I think there's a fifteen hour time difference between here and Pakistan. So, as far as time goes, this is yesterday. If you see what I mean." She paused. "No, you probably don't. It sounds silly enough to my own ears. Perhaps I should check into that consecutive time theory after all."

He wasn't going to be put off. "You were based in Pakistan?"

She began to nod, then stopped suddenly, as if it made her feel dizzy. "Yup. Recently, I was. On water-pump detail. I suppose that doesn't make any sense to you either."

It didn't. "Want to explain?"

"More importantly, do you really want to hear about all this now? Most likely you'll find it deadly dull, and it's certainly not the right topic for a literary dinner anyway."

He wasn't buying that either. "Go on. What's water-pump detail?"

She shrugged, almost as if she knew the answer would be of no importance to him. "It just depends on the situation. At the moment, it's pumping water out of flood areas, but usually, it means getting clean water to the billions of people who have no access to it. In so many communities, drinking water is contaminated with ammonia, phosphate, iron, arsenic, and e-coli, and the only good water is in the hands of a few wealthy landowners who demand huge sums of money for it."

"So what do you do about it?"

"We bring in pumps, put them in the public domain. Supposedly the situation is freed up after that." The corners of the austere mouth tensed.

"Supposedly?"

She looked down at the table, touched the rim of her wine glass. "The problem is, the wealthy land owners usually take over those pumps, too. They're the ones with power and weapons, so there we are: right back in square one." Her delicate fingers waved in a vague gesture of defeat.

"Frustrating."

"Infuriating, more like."

"And dangerous, I imagine."

"Absolutely."

"Are you often in danger?"

"Often enough. But it's part of the job. Aid workers run the risk of gastro-intestinal illness, tropical disease, heat stroke, infected blood transfusions, muggings, and violent attacks. Things are getting worse too because now we're being targeted by suicide bombers and rebel groups who want to stop food supplies or get ransom money. More than a hundred and fifty of us die every year, another hundred and fifty are very badly injured, and even more are kidnapped." She shrugged again. "I happen to be one of the lucky ones."

Marek stared at her, at the earnest expression on her face. He could feel the intensity, the passion when she spoke, despite her attempt to keep up a casual façade. What else had she talked about this evening? She'd made a reference to Belgrade. About once having brought supplies to the opposition. Bosnia had been mentioned, too. A life full of unusual stories.

"You've been doing this sort of thing for a long time?"

"Since I left Paris. Years and years ago." A mocking smile twisted her features. "I never did get over that sixties idealism, you see. Which is what put an end to my marriage." Her eyes met his, squarely.

Was she waiting for him to challenge her? No way he was going to do that! Who was he to criticize what was evidently of utmost importance to her? All he wanted was to know what made her tick, who she was, who she'd become. He needed to solve the mystery.

"Okay. We're making a move."

"Out." She nodded. He could feel the relief flooding through her, tidal-wave style. "That's beautiful music to my ears, Marek Sumner."

"Beautiful ears." His eyes touched hers, and he reached out, caressed the delicate lobe that peeked out from under her heavy hair.

They both liked the contact. Marek reached down, linked her fingers through his, smiled at her through half-closed lids.

Then pulled back. It felt too good, this contact. This isn't what he wanted. It wasn't. Not really. It was great seeing her. It was great being beside her. But he wasn't going to let things get too intimate. Not this time around. Not again.

She hadn't noticed his withdrawal. She only looked happy because they were going off somewhere together. It was going to take some time before they managed to extricate themselves, true—the street outside of this room seemed as far away as the Great Wall of China—but suddenly that didn't seem to matter one little bit, he decided. Because he would be walking out the door with Felicity.

"We need to call a taxi," he said to Carl.

"A taxi," she murmured. "Cinderella's bright orange coach and seven horses wouldn't sound half so romantic. Funny how relative things can be."

Then, sometime in the haze of good-byes and handshakes and invitations and rain checks, the taxi arrived. Marek slipped his arm around her shoulders as they stepped off the curb. It felt good having her there. Very good. Just right. Although Felicity looked as though she were sleepwalking. Still the perfection of this moment didn't escape him. A deep fog had rolled in from the sea, covering the dark city with a salty, calm blanket. Mixed with the tang was the warm, incredibly subtle, marvelously heady scent of Felicity's skin.

"Good to be here," she murmured.

He didn't answer, but he felt his muscles tighten pleasurably in response.

"Where to?" asked the taxi driver.

"The Dupont Hotel," instructed Marek.

"A hotel?"

"That's where I'm staying."

"Oh. I don't have a room," Felicity mumbled, idiotically.

"Of course you don't." Marek's voice was dry. "If you did, you wouldn't be dragging this bag around with you." He indicated the bulky thing on the floor of the cab.

"I think I'll stop making the effort to think. My brain doesn't seem to be a very effective tool at the moment."

He laughed. "Fine. I'll take care of everything."

"Good. It feels nice, having all the decisions made for me, for once. It doesn't happen all that often in my life. Or, when it does, it isn't necessarily positive."

"Meaning what?"

"That I've had years of experience fighting obstreperous officials, well-meaning interfering souls, less well-meaning manipulators, and down-right egotistical maniacs with machine guns in their hands."

A life so different from his own; a life spent on another planet altogether. Now what? He didn't know her. Not anymore. She, Felicity, as familiar to him as his own skin, was also as distant as the moon. So what would happen in the hotel room? What would he do with her? One room or two, he wondered. Was he even going to ask her if she wanted to sleep in the same bed he did? Did he even want to share a bed with this ghost from the past? He did. Very much. But did she?

She hadn't protested when he'd invited her back to his hotel, had she? She hadn't resisted, and she was certainly wise enough to know men didn't invite women to hotel rooms for a quiet chat and a coffee. But he wondered if he was making a terrible mistake, insisting on this intimacy. The thought even made him angry—angry for putting them both in this situation. What, exactly, had he been thinking of? Having a quick fling? He felt ashamed. Because he'd given her no choice. Given himself no alternative.

And was he willing to take chances again? He'd had his heart broken once before by Felicity. What did he expect this time around? A few days of passion before she waved goodbye again? Yes, that would be it. Off she'd go, hopping from one plane to another, heading back to some hellhole. Some new water-pump ordeal.

Try and keep things cool, Sumner, he warned himself. You aren't a starry-eyed twenty-two-year-old now. Keep things easy this time, the way you would with any old friend. Keep away from the undertow.

The taxi turned left, joined the avenue that led away from the sea and the road south. Familiar. All of this was so familiar...

"Marek?" She was leaning forward now, peering through the window of the cab out into the night. "Marek, look!"

He looked. What was there to see? What was so important out there? This was just another wide, dark avenue with large, looming houses outlined against the night. A pleasant middle class neighborhood, most likely. Nothing more.

"Marek. Don't tell me you've forgotten." There was a wide-awake urgency in her voice. "Don't you remember that garden?" She began to laugh. "Look. It's one of these. There. That one." Her pointing finger indicated a picket fence, a dense tangle of shrubbery.

A memory clicked into place. "The trip to Mexico!"

"The *planned* trip to Mexico."

"And this was the farthest we got."

"No one picked us up. All day we stood there, hitching."

"In the heat."

Backpacks beside them, the sun searing down. They had, on the spur of the moment, decided to head south. To Mexico. Felicity had said she knew it well: he, Marek, knew nothing. Felicity had spoken of a turquoise bay, not far from the border. She'd talked about a mixture of strange, juicy black clams floating in shrimp broth mixed with onions and chili peppers that were strong enough to make a macho—or a feminist— cry. Tomatoes chopped finely, sweet and crunchy chunks of onion, perfumed coriander leaves.

"Marek. You have to try it. Life isn't worth living until you have." Pleasure first, that was Felicity, all right.

He'd let himself be convinced, permitted himself to be lured away from books and papers. Of course. He usually did give in to Felicity—after a brief struggle, naturally. That enthusiasm of hers could carry away whole armies if ever the chance arose.

Except no one had given them a ride. It was holiday time, the worst period for hitching anywhere.

The cars had been full of squabbling children and their exasperated, suspicious looking parents. You could see the mistrust—and hatred on their faces as they drove by.

"Dirty hippies! Go get yourselves decent jobs! Earn money to buy your own car!"

"How long are we going to stand here like this?" Marek had felt foolish. He didn't like being the object of scorn. The abandoned books and papers waiting for him on his desk took on more appeal with every passing second.

"And you're ready to quit? Come on, Marek. Think of beautiful, fresh tortillas, just hot off the griddle. Imagine peppers stuffed with cheese that melts onto your fork."

They'd ended up sitting on a low, crumbling wall over-looking the sea on the outskirts of San Francisco, eating the avocado and alfalfa sprout sandwiches Felicity had prepared for the voyage. Sandwiches meant to be consumed somewhere further south, "in the red-neck belt, where we probably won't even get served coffee in a diner because you have long hair!"

It had been dark by the time they'd begun the trudge back to Haight-Ashbury.

"So much for your Mexican paradise."

"Sleeping on the beach. Making love under the stars." She'd laughed. "Actually, that was one of the main reasons I wanted to go."

"Making love in a bed isn't good enough?"

"Oh, it's good enough, all right." Her eyes were wicked, taunting. They seemed to glow in the night. "But I have this image, here." She pointed to her head. "I see you naked. All smooth and cool stretched out under the stars. And I think of all the things I'm going to do to you. The way I'm going to taste you." Her voice was hot, lazy, full of promise. She'd run her fingers down over his shoulder, skimming down over his chest, down, slowly down to where his thighs joined. There she'd felt the hard, pulsing evidence of exactly how nice her promises sounded to him, too.

The garden had been so inviting. They'd climbed over the fence, giggling, whispering. A rose garden, large, almost invisible from the house. The perfume of the flowers weighed heavy on the sullen night air. They had rolled out their sleeping bags with barely suppressed mirth and many *sotto voce* comments about what they'd say when the police arrested them.

Then, humor slipped out of the picture. She'd been right. There was something to be said for moonlight and the secret darkness of night. There was an extra enticement in standing naked to the skies. For a minute he'd stood still, watching her, etched in pale lunar beams, a fairy goddess, an object of desire. He loosened the barrettes that held her hair, and it tumbled down, dark, perfumed drifts curling over her shoulders and down her back.

When he drew her into his arms, her breath became a sigh and she moaned out his name. He'd cupped her beautiful breasts in his hands, then lowered his head to take the rosy nipples in his mouth. She'd arched desperately against him, leading him on with her hips, her belly.

Make love under the stars? That was what she'd wanted, and that's what she was going to get.

Only he was the one who was calling the shots. He was the one who would taste and tease, delight and capture. He would love her all night long, have her stretched beneath him, pale, glowing and wanting only him.

And what if he stopped this taxi now? Now. Some forty-odd years later? *What if we climbed back over that fence tonight? Would she even come with me? Would she agree?* Would the reality of today live up to that memory of passion?

Nonsense. Antics like those belonged to youth. Or to a relationship. This was not a relationship. This was a chance meeting—almost. True, chance had played a certain role. Then Felicity had taken the rest into her capable hands. That was Felicity, all right. Leave nothing up to good luck. If you want something, then just go after it: that had always been her theory.

The taxi turned again, headed into the heart of the city. The garden was far behind them. The moment also. They were back to today. Nothing to regret, Marek, he told himself. And quashed the feeling of something having been irrevocably lost.

****

It was a small, elegant hotel. A sleepy night porter shuffled through a dimly lit lobby, opened the door to let them in. They took the elevator to the third floor.

Room 306, Felicity thought sleepily. *I'm going to etch this one on my memory.* Little things like that seemed to be of utmost importance. And here she was, finally alone with Marek. Finally.

The evening had seemed endless. She'd felt as though she'd been sitting at that dinner table for a century and a half. At first it had been fun. Stimulating. Then exhaustion had gotten the better of her. Didn't anyone want to go home? If she'd spent the evening running along a treadmill in hell, she couldn't have felt worse. A treadmill. No conceivable end in sight.

She could have left, found a hotel, a bed, some place to curl up in, get some sleep. Sleep? The idea was almost too luxurious to even contemplate.

And there had been one major complication: Marek. She hadn't been prepared to get up and leave, just like that. Say: "Good night, sweet dreams, it was great seeing you again." If she'd done so, then Marek might have vanished out of her life again. She couldn't take the risk. No way on earth she'd take the risk. Whatever happened, she had to stay near him.

Now, here she was. In a beautiful, airy, old-fashioned hotel room with Marek. Transparent white curtains billowed faintly at an open window; dark brown elegant furniture glowed. This room bespoke luxury, class. She hadn't seen anything approaching it in donkey's years. Then there was the bed. A large, wonderful-looking bed. One bed. They were going to sleep in one bed! Unless one of them was going to take up residence on the carpet…which didn't seem likely. Or perhaps she didn't even want to think about that possibility. Not now. She didn't dare.

But now that they were alone, the intimacy of the situation was intimidating.

"You're going to go to sleep immediately," Marek ordered her. "You're wiped out." Was he aware of her uncertainty, or was he simply being solicitous? Did it even matter? It was heaven, being ordered around by him.

Her lips curved into a smile. "No way. First I'm having a shower. The last time I did, I was on the other side of the world, standing in a straw hut. As a matter of fact, you probably wouldn't even have recognized it as a shower. Inside the hut was a plastic bottle with holes punched into the bottom and filled with cold water. I had about sixty seconds to clean up. After that, the price went up a dollar."

He laughed, his eyes playing over her, and her heart jumped. If only she didn't feel so confused when she was with him she might be able to work out what was happening. She saw his gaze flutter over her lips, saw him shift, closing in the space separating them. The heat rose deep inside her body.

He's going to kiss me, she thought, and the idea created chaos in her mind. He's going to come over here, stand here right in front of me, bend down, and kiss me. Her lips burned with anticipation. She waited.

Then, abruptly, his expression changed. Closed down. He turned away from her, pretended to be busy with papers on the desk.

Now what?

He hadn't kissed her. He hadn't, although he might as well have. The sensation was there at the corners of her mouth, in the depths of her belly. She remembered how it felt, his mouth on hers, his body touching hers. So why had he turned away like that? Disappointment raced through her veins.

"Okay. Shower's in there." Keeping his voice level, cool, he indicated a door on their left. "No plastic bottle with holes. As much hot water as you'd like."

"Right!" She forced herself to smile brightly despite the sinking feeling. The secret moment was over. It had been there for a second: want. And need. Flashing between them, bright as a blinding strobe light.

And, just as quickly, it had gone.

Still, she couldn't have misread the signals. Intensity: he'd felt it, just like she had. And he'd rejected it. He didn't want her, after all. He didn't want to feel anything as far as she was concerned. That was all in the past. Long over with.

Get into that shower!

The hot water felt wonderful as it gushed over her, although it didn't clean out the ache of his rejection. That was going to hang around for some time. Unless she managed to get control of herself, her emotions. Cool herself down. Resign herself to a nice warm friendship with Marek. She didn't know if she was equal to the task.

Then you're just going to have to seduce the hell out of him. If possible...

She felt even more doubtful about her chances of doing just that when she stepped out of the shower and came back into the room. He was standing at the window staring down at the street: tall, hard-muscled, his shoulders powerful. She caught sight of his profile, etched against the sky. A sculptured face, the straight, imperious nose. A million miles away. And thinking of someone else? Regretting she was here? She pushed the ugly thoughts to the back of her mind.

"Uh—Marek?"

He turned, his eyes sweeping over her, taking in the thick, white towel fastened, sarong style, over her slender curves, and she felt her heartbeat increase again, sending tension along every single nerve. *Cut this out.* This is nothing but pure, potent sexuality. Which was difficult enough at the best of times.

"Yes?"

"I don't have a nightgown, pajamas, anything." If anything sounded like provocation, that sure did. He must think she was coming on strong. A frustrated old thing creeping out of the shrubbery. She felt the embarrassed blush as it crept into her cheeks. "I mean, I just threw things into my bag. I had less than an hour before getting back out to the airport in Germany."

"Pakistan. Germany." His lips twitched. "Mars? Jupiter?"

Her chin tilted defiantly. "That sounds like a criticism."

His face softened, as if the defiance had touched him. "That's the Felicity I know. Exhausted, coming from places that I only read about, you're still ready for a fight."

"I don't mean to sound like a crank."

"Did I say you did?"

Why was she arguing? She only wished he would cross the room, pull back the towel covering her still damp body, run his hands over her skin, taste her. "Sorry."

"You really have changed from the old days." His eyes glinted humorously.

"What's that supposed to mean?" She shot suspicion back at him again.

"Not having a nightgown. Since when did that ever bother you?"

"Why I—" She stopped, confused, then saw he was laughing. Of course. The old Felicity would never have worried about anything so prudish. Not with Marek. She'd wanted him, had set out to get him, had made all the moves—and suffered the rejections when they came. This was old, familiar territory. Well, it wasn't going to happen that way now! He was going to have to make the proposals. She could wait.

"Fine." She shrugged. "Just warning you." She headed for the bed, too conscious of his eyes as they followed her, too conscious of questions left hanging in the air.

Now what? Did she whip off the towel, stand there in front of him naked, exposed to his rejection? What was he going to think about her forty-years-older body?

She glanced up, almost fearfully, and saw he'd politely turned away. Being polite. Yes, that was Marek, all right. Tactfully trying not to let it show he didn't want her, not really.

She slid between the soft sheets and closed her eyes. "Lord, this is heaven," she breathed.

"We should have left Carl's earlier. Why didn't you say anything?"

And risked losing you? The concern in his voice reached out to her. "Isn't heaven nicer when you have to wait a long time for it?" But she didn't feel like sparring. She only wanted sleep now. She couldn't fight that any longer. Sleep. That's what she needed. Almost as much as she needed the feel of his body on hers.

Well, you can't have everything you want in life. Take what you can and simply do without the rest.

Negative thoughts. Ones that trot in on the heels of exhaustion.

Why did he continue to stand over there by the window as if afraid to approach? She meant to ask him, meant to accuse him of not wanting to come to bed because she was in it. But drowsiness curled over her, carried her away softly.

Leaving him watching her, noting the soft lashes

fringing her closed eyes, the untamed tangle of silvery hair fanning across the pillow.

Slowly he undressed, slid into the bed beside her. Sound asleep, like an exhausted child. Some child! She looked...sexy! Sensuous! Irresistible...almost.

Her breathing was regular. She probably didn't even know he was here, beside her. Gently, he slipped one arm around her shoulders, pulled her into his warmth. Her breasts pressed against his chest; her breath whispered softly on his neck. Desire woke again, deep down in his belly. *What the hell are you doing? You must be crazy.* He considered moving away, protecting himself from feelings that threatened his every effort to remain calm and removed.

Yet he didn't want to wake her.

And he didn't want to stop touching her, holding her in his arms.

"Sleep well, beautiful Felicity," he murmured softly, and she stirred in her sleep, a faint smile flitting over her mouth, almost as if she'd heard.

He moaned with frustration. It was going to be a long night. He wondered if there would be any sleep in it for him.

Chapter Six

When she woke, she didn't have the faintest idea where she was. The country, the circumstance, the day, the corner of the world, all that escaped her. *Split second amnesia. Or just the usual muddle?* Then, memory came searing in.

San Francisco. Marek! Her eyes flew open.

Rays of gaudy sunshine danced merrily across the huge, rumpled bed. She was alone. Marek had gone!

Where? When? She sat up, blinking in the bright light. What time could it possibly be? Where had Marek slept? Not beside her. Surely not.

Yet there, hovering on the edge of her consciousness, was a faint, hazy impression of having lain in his arms. Of, sometime in the night, having felt his lips on her forehead, kissing her softly as if he didn't want to wake her, didn't want her to know...

Fact or fantasy? *Wishful thinking most likely.* Or, perhaps not. The pillow next to hers showed where a head had lain. He'd been here. Right here, in the bed beside her.

And she'd gone and slept through it! Something that might never happen again. Fool!

Perhaps he won't be back, whispered the voice of panic.

She stared around her. Of course he would. There was his shirt, thrown across a chair. His leather case was by the window.

Perhaps he'd left in order to give her a chance to get out of the room, leave the hotel without their having to meet up again? A gentle way of letting her save face after he'd refused to kiss her, make love with her. Perhaps she was exaggerating? No. He'd made it perfectly clear. He didn't want her or, worse yet, he *had* wanted her, and then, for some obscure reason, he'd changed his mind.

So why had he invited her back here, to his room? Would they be together here tonight? Her heart began pounding at the very thought. Maybe tonight he'd hold her in his arms. Maybe tonight she'd feel his mouth against hers. Maybe tonight he'd say, yes, they were meant to be together. After all these years. That their separation had only been a brief pause along life's road, a pause in which to gather stories and experiences. A pause in which you discovered what you really wanted. Oh, wouldn't that be wonderful.

Tonight she wouldn't fall asleep. This time he wouldn't be able to resist her. She wanted him, heart, soul and body. Nothing else mattered.

But what if things didn't happen that way? What if last night had been their only one together? What if he came back this morning and said he wanted to be alone? What if he told her he was in love with another woman? What if...

Stop this immediately! Stop agonizing.

She sank back against the pillows, tried to stop her thoughts swirling around in such a negative way. What difference did it make whether Marek was in her life or not? Honestly! She'd built this meeting up in her mind, had let it grow all out of proportion. *Stop worrying.*

Relax! She forced herself to stretch her long, supple limbs, squeeze the tension out of them. Marek or no Marek, life went on.

It would just be so much nicer if...

The door suddenly clicked open, and Marek walked into the room. Felicity let out her breath with a whoosh of relief.

"It's you!"

A smile tugged at his fine mouth, and the corners of his eyes crinkled. "Were you expecting someone else?" His voice was light, teasing. He was dressed in nut-colored, corduroy trousers that hugged his long thighs, and his white shirt seemed, for some reason, to accentuate the deep sea-green of his eyes. She wouldn't have minded looking at him without all those clothes either. She made a vague attempt to shove the wicked thoughts to the back of her mind. Failed.

Stop drooling.

He'd shaved, she noticed. Last night's faint shadowing was gone. His cheek would feel nice against hers. There was a soft, soapy smell that clung to his skin, skin she wanted to lick.

She sat up, carefully keeping the sheet tucked against her nakedness. "No. Of course I wasn't expecting anyone else!" When their eyes touched, she felt her body quiver, almost as if the contact had been physical. "I was simp—" She stopped abruptly, catching sight of a flash of color in his hand.

He was holding a rose. One perfect red rose. For her. Just like the one he'd held out to her so many years ago, after the first, almost unbelievable night they'd spent together.

That was why he hadn't been here when she'd

woken. He'd gone to fetch her a rose! He had never forgotten!

The lump in her throat was so big, she doubted she'd ever be able to speak in whole sentences again. She hated the tears that rushed into her eyes. "Oh, Marek!"

"Good morning, Felicity."

"Why?" she whispered, her heart in those words.

He sat down beside her on the bed. "Because I couldn't have resisted if I'd wanted to," he answered with honesty. "Look, Felicity. The rose is just for old time's sake. Memory lane. That's all. Don't take it too seriously."

"Don't take it seriously?" Who was he kidding? Was he playing with her? She swallowed and tried to glue a bright smile on her face, tried to stop the tears sliding down her cheeks.

"Sorry," she said swiping away at the tears. And feeling ridiculous.

Briefly, he bent toward her, kissed her forehead. As if she were a child. "Tell me, how do you feel about breakfast these days?" His voice was light. Impersonal. "As I recall, you were always ravenous in the morning."

"Still am." She forced herself to laugh back at him. Hungry? Was he kidding? How in heaven's name could she feel hungry at a moment like this? She'd probably never feel hungry again in her life. It was incredible how he remembered little things like their breakfasts. Like so much else, such fine detail had been part of the web of their life together.

"How about if I call room service. Coffee? Eggs? Toast? The works?"

"The works." She was going to force herself to eat, act casual, even if it killed her—which it most likely would. "What time is it anyway?" Why did she always seem to be asking that same question? What did it matter?

"Ten. And outside the sun is shining. The weather is perfect. You know for what?"

She caught the gleam in his eyes and shook her head slowly. "No. Tell me."

"A walk."

"A walk?" For the space of a few seconds, she could do nothing but stare, her mind reeling. A walk! Just like back then. Just like when she'd come to his apartment for the first time! "Through the city?"

"Through the city." He nodded. "Through the Haight, down Geary."

"With ice cream?"

"You think it still exists, the homemade ice cream?"

"We'll find out." She nodded with assurance. Why was it so damned important to her that it did?

"We will. Then there's the visit to a gallery."

"A gallery? What kind of gallery? An art gallery?"

"You remember Nick Quinte, don't you?"

"Nick Quinte! Painter of psychedelic roses and saucer-eyed LSD angels!"

"Apparently he's made a name for himself. He's all the rage here in San Francisco. There's a show of his on at the moment."

"Angels?" She scrunched up her features.

"I doubt it. But we'll find out soon enough. After a long, luxurious lunch. How does that sound? I'm richer these days." There was a faintly mocking edge to his voice. "No more student budget."

"Will it be as wonderful with the new luxury added?" The wistful note crept in despite herself.

"Maybe," he said, watching her closely. "Maybe it will even be better."

"Maybe." She kept her voice steady although it was the last thing she was feeling now. She felt like jumping to her feet and dancing. Clicking her heels together. Clapping. Shouting for joy. She would have this whole day with Marek. Then the evening. And the night. Time enough to seduce him, to charm him. Yes, things were going to be all right, after all. She knew it in her heart of hearts.

Didn't she?

Or are you just letting your dreams carry you away to some lush, green world of perfect happiness? A world that can't possibly exist outside of your crazy head.

****

The gallery was chic, undeniably fashionable, perfectly in tune with what was going on in the field of contemporary art.

"Are you sure this isn't the wrong place?" Felicity whispered. "It looks as though we're in the middle of a construction site—or an eventual construction site."

A site where neither the architect nor the builders had the faintest idea what they were going to do, Marek thought. He looked at the red bricks lined up along one wall and facing another red row lined up in the middle of the gallery floor.

"Here a brick, there a brick, everywhere a brick-brick." Felicity peered at the work's title on a card. "Exercise One, it's called."

"That helps us out," Marek replied, his face poker straight.

"Makes you really itchy to see what Exercise Two or Three are all about, doesn't it?" she murmured quietly.

Not quietly enough. An incredibly bored young man with an incredibly fashionable haircut threw her an agonized look from behind an incredibly long, black lacquer desk. "Perhaps you need some guidance?" His voice indicated Felicity needed more than that.

"You can bet your booties I do. I've been out in the sticks for years." She smiled good-naturedly, and Marek repressed a wild urge to laugh.

Languidly, the man uncurled himself from an extraordinary cowhide and scrap metal chair—a reject left behind by Martian spaceship—and crossed to where Marek and Felicity were standing. Then he turned, gestured to the bricks.

"The work is all about the modalities of the relationship between affiliation and territory." He paused dramatically.

Felicity's smile spread into an even more affable grin. "Well, that's certainly a cute start."

Marek prodded her with his elbow. But he was having fun. He really was. The way her face shone, the note of suppressed laughter in her voice. A warm glow spread throughout his body. This was good. Really good.

"And the proximity of borders," continued the young man, determined to ignore Felicity totally. "The multiplicity of borders produce superposed currents in artistic thought and in the imaginary it triggers there and elsewhere."

"Especially elsewhere." She nodded with what—almost—looked like enthusiasm. More like pure delight.

He was going to have to get her out of there, Marek decided. Fast. Before she got them arrested for insolence. "Of course the general problem can't really fit a systematic analysis of the exhibited work," he interposed calmly.

There was an extended silence.

Felicity decided to fill the gap. "It's a right change from the angels Nick used to do, multiplicity of borders, no multiplicity of borders."

"Angels?" questioned the elegant young man with a bored twitch of a left eyebrow.

"When I knew him, Nick was into painting angels. Green ones, pink ones. Multiplicity of angels, you might say. Or perhaps a simple multitude?"

"Felicity. You need an ice cream." Marek took her elbow firmly and led toward the door.

Meekly, she let herself be led. "Right you are, Marek. With multifarious flavors."

"I thought you only ate chocolate and vanilla."

She stopped dead, stared at him with astonishment. Blinked.

"What's wrong?"

"Marek? You remember *that* after all these years? That I only like vanilla and chocolate? For over forty years, you keep that in your mind?"

He felt like laughing at himself. He felt like running away. He certainly didn't feel like answering and didn't even know if he could. So he hedged. "You said multifarious. So I thought you'd changed."

She'd noticed the hedging, but knew she couldn't

push him, ruin what was happening between them…despite his reticence. The air sparkled; there was complicity.

"Is two too puny a number for a grandiose word like multifarious?" she asked.

The ice cream shop had been converted into a video shop; the little park where they'd formerly sat had been turned into a playground with ugly, fiberglass cartoon characters. They crossed into Turk street, found what they were looking for: homemade ice cream. It wasn't such an unusual thing to find in San Francisco after all. Not even these days.

They each ordered two scoops.

"Worried about your waistline?" Felicity taunted him. "You were always a man of excess when it came to ice cream. Apricot, blueberry, chocolate chip, and mint." So she remembered that, too. It was…uncanny.

"Not worried about my waistline," he said, slightly miffed. "I'm simply leaving room for my dinner. I've been invited to Myra's this evening."

"Myra's? You're going to My-rah's house for dinner?" Felicity stopped eating her ice cream— chocolate and vanilla, of course—in mid-lick, stared at Marek with astonishment. Or was it pure disappointment? Real or feigned astonishment? Real or feigned disappointment? Marek wasn't certain. There always had been—still was—a certain air of high drama about Felicity. She'd never been able to talk about something, even something as banal as the weather, without wild gestures, an excited tone of voice. She'd always had that need for exaggerated reaction, for theatrics. Did he approve? Marek wasn't certain. It was certainly a contrast to the everyday politeness and calm self-control normally encountered in human relationships. Still, did one need all the high drama?

Or was he just looking for reasons to disapprove of Felicity? Trying to find excuses not to get involved. He was having too much fun, just at the moment. He liked seeing her delicate face as the emotions played over it. He liked strolling through the streets beside her, here in the bright sun, in the glowing almost liquid heat of the city. Was it Felicity herself who glowed? What if he missed her too much when they split up again? Like he had the last time, back then, in Paris.

Even worse, was he trying to hide what he'd felt early this morning while he watched her sleep? Hide it from her, perhaps. He couldn't hide it from himself. Curls that caressed the white of the pillow. The mouth, the wonderful, narrow mouth relaxed into softness. The jagged rush of desire had seared through him, so sharp it was almost painful. He'd wanted to allow himself to take her again, in just the same way he had forty years ago.

She was naked under those covers. Her long, lean body was there, waiting for his caresses. He knew she wanted them. He knew her long, slanting eyes would open slowly, wondering, pleased, before the heat of her pleasure filled them anew.

And he'd forced himself to move away. To think of other things. Cool thoughts. Breakfast, for example. Or ice cream. Ice cream? That made him think of her delicate tongue, now licking the cool, icy cone.

No! Not thoughts like that, he told himself. He watched her, saw the emotions as they played across her face, emotions that touched him more deeply than he'd ever expected. He fought against his reaction, fought against his need. Cursed himself for being a fool.

Bringing her a rose this morning! He'd only done it because of that old memory, and he'd made a mess of things. Let her think romance was in the cards again. That they would take up just where they'd left off. Impossible! Absolutely, perfectly impossible. He'd see to it. Because he'd changed: he was a loner, now. He needed solitude. Freedom. Silence. Definitely not a relationship. So the rose had been a bad mistake. But not irremediable.

Or had it been? He'd seen her tears. They'd torn into his gut, but he'd told himself he shouldn't let himself feel like that. But he had. What was it he'd wanted to do? He'd wanted to bend down, plant soft, butterfly kisses on her eyelids, on her wet face, taste the sweet saltiness of her tears. Close his fists in the warm, sexy, wild tangle of her hair.

Wanted. And did nothing. Because he wouldn't be able to stop. He'd been too excruciatingly aware only a thin strip of linen separated him from her body. He'd seen the slow rise and fall of her breasts, and knew if he made love to her, it would be astonishing. Just as it had been before.

But he wasn't going to. Despite his desire. Because he knew every thought should be on self-preservation, and not on possessing her.

"Yes, I'm going to Myra's house for dinner," he answered now, his voice dry. A tone meant to discourage any further comment on this particular subject. Why was he feeling so defensive?

"God. That'll be exciting," Felicity muttered, her voice thick with sarcasm.

Marek looked at her sharply. "I can't believe this. You are still capable of being catty about Myra after forty-three years? What's she ever done to you?"

"Nothing." Felicity contemplated her ice cream with intense concentration. "This vanilla is seriously starting to melt."

Fascinated, Marek again watched her pink cat's tongue catch a tiny rivulet seconds before it reached her long fingers. "Why have you always seen Myra as an enemy? Why are you being catty?" She seemed determined not to meet his eyes. But he knew, too well, she was being eaten alive by jealousy.

"Oh, Marek!" Felicity waved her left hand, an impatient, exasperated gesture. "It's perfectly obvious. Myra hates me. Myra hates everything I represent. She feels I put her entire life into doubt. And she's wrong. I don't care how she lives. Why can't she just be liberal enough to allow me the same privilege?"

"Can't you see you're one of the strong people in the world," Marek said quietly. "You've always had the fearlessness, the confidence to do what you wanted in life."

"Or the blind stupidity," Felicity muttered. "You're reading me all wrong."

Marek laughed shortly. "No. I'm not. And, believe me, the Myras of this world need nothing more than security. They're frightened. And jealous of people like you who take risks."

"Therefore they don't approve. They want everyone to fall into line. To be as terrified as they are."

"Do you always have to have approval?" Marek's brow furrowed.

"Did you see the looks she was sending me over

the table last night? As if hoping I'd dissolve." Felicity straightened up, met Marek's eyes defiantly. "And by the way, yes. I do need approval. I know I can't have it from every single human in the whole world, but that just happens to be the way I function. I want everyone to like me. I want to make everyone laugh—or at least smile."

"And do you manage?" Of course she did! Why did he even doubt it? He hoped the nasty tug he was feeling had nothing to do with jealousy. And how many other men had felt just the same way over the last forty-odd years? He pushed the thought of those men out of his mind. What did they have to do with him?

"Why are you looking so hostile?" she asked. "And yes, sometimes I do manage to get people to smile. Not always, of course." Her eyes questioned his with wry amusement. "You don't approve either, I see."

"Approve? What does my approval have to do with anything?" His voice was gruff. "I suppose most of us are content to blend in with the crowd." Which was true. Life was easier that way.

His talent lay in writing down words. A lonely job. A solitary one. But if you'd been born with waving red hair, you automatically stood out. Even when the red had become a wild and beautiful tangle of shining silver. Her eyes! The way they glittered. Sometimes mischievous. Sometimes provocative. He could stare at her all day long, watch, with fascination, the play of emotions, the sparkle.

Then fall into the same old trap: wanting and not being able to capture her. Who could capture a glitter? He didn't want to go through all the pain again. It was far better to remain friends with Felicity. Pain? He didn't need pain in his well-organized, well-modulated life. He'd learnt that in Paris.

"That's what you said to me in Paris," she said.

Paris? Now she was reading his mind! Paris. That was a time he didn't want to conjure up again. It was a moment he wanted to forget.

"Do we have to bring this up?" He stood. Began walking.

"Bring what up? Paris?" She stood, too. Followed him as he set out down Geary. "Of course we should bring up what happened in Paris. It's part of our history."

And part of their problem. Also a total disaster.

****

A rainy November in 1974. And cold. Why had he shown up? In order to show her the error of her ways? To convince her to return to San Francisco and what she thought was mediocrity!

She'd been living in an old fashioned apartment on the rue du Chateau near Montparnasse, an apartment she shared with three French men. Three men and Felicity! It was outrageous. He remembered seeing them. Two art students and a passionate, gentle, burgeoning playwright. All three men had been fresh faced, good-looking, and obviously fascinated by her. He remembered wondering which one was in love with her. All of them were, no doubt. Did she care about them, too?

"Of course I'm the center of attention," she'd said with defiance, a toss of her head, a blazing challenge in her eyes. "And I'm having fun. An incredible amount of fun." Meaning when she'd been living with him, in San Francisco, life had been anything but fun. Isn't that what she was saying? Or was he so busy lacerating himself, he couldn't think straight.

The sidewalks had been gray and dirty, the trees bare, their branches stretched out bleakly toward the gloomy sky. Had he really thought he could convince her she needed him? That her life was uninteresting without him?

"You sell chestnuts on the street?" He was incredulous, condescending. And sneering. Everything he shouldn't have been.

"It's fun, selling chestnuts! I talk to people. I get to observe everyone. And I've learnt to speak decent French. Well, sort of." She'd laughed, her cheeks were rosy in the cutting wind. "My accent is atrocious!"

What did he care if it was? All he wanted was for her to return. To wait for him, wait until his degree was finished, his thesis written. Yet he couldn't have that. He knew it. She'd put that world behind her—for the time being.

"And exactly where would an excellent French accent get you? Or selling chestnuts, for that matter?"

"You sound like my mother!" Felicity's laugh had been a frosty tinkle, as cold as the wind sliding its chill fingers under the collar of his too-light trench coat.

He'd tried to see things her way. Had tried to find pleasure in the endless evenings spent in cafés—loud, smoky, damp places, their windows streaked with moisture. It had been a failure. Listening to café chit-chat and bright philosophizing in a foreign tongue he found exceedingly hard to follow bored him. And he hated the weather: when it didn't rain, the frozen air never seemed to warm either.

He'd watched her, heard her repartee in the

language he'd started to detest. How she'd glowed. How jealous he'd been! He'd been eaten alive by jealousy. How could she be so easy-going, so happy without him? So ridiculously beautiful, and so distant. Less than a year had passed since she'd left him, yet Felicity was already part of this other world.

"This means you won't be coming back?"

"I want to live!" Her protest was vehement. "Why should I come back? You can write your thesis here too, you know. You have a grant. You can come and live with me in Paris."

"Of course I can't, and you know that." He almost hated her because he wanted her so much. These were final moments. They both knew it.

Then there had been the last good-bye at the train station. Buffeted by a bitter wind that never let up, he stood, suitcase in hand, waiting for the bus to take him to the airport.

"You'll write to me?" Her eyes begged.

He'd shrugged, as if it made no difference to him. "Perhaps." He wouldn't write to her, of course. He'd been abandoned by her, and there was no way he'd reward her for it. No, she'd never hear from him again.

****

"Do you have to walk so quickly?" Felicity's voice prodded him back into the present. To here. To this bright, sunny San Francisco afternoon, four decades later.

Traffic roared around them. Somewhere ahead lay the glittering bay. Tall buildings had grown up into the hot city air. It was a big, busy city now—and it had seemed so calm and provincial back then. Even to him. Yes, times had changed. Life had gone on. He wasn't still angry, was he? After all this time?

"Sorry." He was. He hadn't realized how large his steps had been, how hurried. As if trying to run away from memories that hurt. His eyes flickered down to the worn out ballerina shoes Felicity wore. She wouldn't complain, he knew, but walking couldn't be easy in shoes like that. Didn't she have money? How did she live? The questions were too personal to ask after such a short time together. She was a stranger.

He slowed his pace. "Whatever happened to the three of them?"

Felicity looked up, eyes puzzled. "The three of them?"

"The men you shared that apartment with in Paris! All of them were so determined to be great artists. Did they make it?"

Her grin was broad, good-humored. "Not really. Marcel never became a playwright after all. He went into the family business. And Jean-Paul went into sales. Christian worked in advertising."

"So much for great ideals."

"Didn't Gustave Flaubert say that every bourgeois, in the flame of his youth, believes himself capable of immense passion?"

He was still feeling bitter. What a ridiculous joke! And he didn't want to talk about Flaubert, either. "They were all in love with you, weren't they?"

"Who knows? Fascinated, certainly. You were terribly jealous, weren't you? At least, I hoped you were."

"Why?"

"Because I felt that you rejected the person I was. That you wanted to make me into something I wasn't.

You wanted to stifle me."

She was right, in a way. He wouldn't have wanted to stifle the person she was, but he'd resented her need to follow her dreams. He'd wanted to settle down, and he'd wanted her to settle down with him. And that had had nothing to do with what she'd wanted in life. Or so she'd said at the time.

"But you did get married."

"And divorced, soon after."

"Tell me about your husband."

"What could you possibly want to know about him?" She was hedging.

"You're the one who believes in asking direct questions, aren't you?"

"It's just not an interesting subject of conversation," she muttered sulkily.

"Oh, yes. For me it is." No way he was going to let her wriggle out of this. She'd refused him all those years ago but had accepted marriage with someone else. He had to know why.

Felicity sighed. "Okay. Here goes. He was a businessman. His name was Pierre Chenot. He was French. Parisian. The perfect member of the good family you once told me I was going to marry into. This is killing me, Marek. Do I have to go on?"

"What's killing you?" His voice betrayed a trickle of laughter.

"Admitting you were right about my eventually getting married to Mr. Perfectly Good Family. Pierre was a company director. Very correct. I met him at a dinner party given by an artist friend. I suppose I interested him because I represented what he thought was the attractive side of 'bohemian' life. The life he'd read about, thought about, dreamed about secretly. An intriguing sort of life he'd never have the nerve to participate in."

"So he picked you as his wife. That way he could be a bohemian, second hand."

"Except that he decided I wasn't supposed to be too original, or too different. Once we were married, I was supposed to go back to being the tame, good girl from a good family again. The one who could organize dinner parties, take the wives of visiting guests to see fashion shows, buy luxury products and perfume."

"Why did you marry him?"

"I don't know, really. I mean, he was good-looking. Pierre was nice and cultured and he did everything to charm me, win me over. And also...well...I guess, as you once said, I had been programmed to marry someone like that. I suppose by then I was feeling that my free and easy life was also a fairly trivial one."

"And it would take on meaning by getting married?"

The look she gave him was half resentful and half mocking. "Of course it wouldn't. I know that *now*. But back then I was young and silly. And bored. And aimless. And inexperienced. Besides, everyone is allowed to make lots and lots of mistakes in life."

"Don't I know that." He nodded. "What about children?"

"No children. I told you forty-some years ago I didn't want children. And then, when I started working in foreign aid programs, there were masses of starving, needy, and unwanted children to take care of. I never did feel the urge or necessity to create my own."

"So how long did it last, your marriage?"

"Almost three whole years." Her mouth curved into a slightly embarrassed smile.

Marek whistled. "That's impressive." He didn't want to sound nasty but the idea of her three-year marriage irritated him. Three years was longer than she'd stayed with him.

"Don't make fun of me. I had a very good reason for getting the hell out."

"Okay. Shoot."

"Well, we'd gone out to dinner with another couple. A couple newly arrived in Paris. The husband was someone in advertising. He'd been transferred from London. It was going to be the usual tedious dinner, you know."

"Tell me."

"The company wives talk about their brilliant children, and the company men jaw on about accounts and clients in these very boring voices."

"Except this time it was different?"

"It was. Because the other wife and I got along. Really well. It took us about three minutes to decide we were going to be the best of friends."

"I can see what's coming. Your husband didn't approve?"

"That's right! You see, he was afraid this other man had been transferred because the company wanted to get rid of him. And if that was so, I couldn't be friends with the wife of someone who was on the long social slide downward. He actually forbade me to call her! Can you imagine?" She stopped. Remembered how angry she'd been at the time.

"So you defied him?"

"You bet I did. I packed a bag and left. Took a bus to Turkey and never came back."

"That's our Felicity. She doesn't do things halfway. Doesn't move to another apartment. Doesn't move in with a girlfriend. She doesn't even have a bloody great argument with hubby. She just jumps on a bus to Turkey." Or onto a plane going to Brussels.

She lifted her head and studied his face. What was he sounding so bitter about? "There had been this terrible earthquake, you see. In Eastern Turkey. And I thought maybe I could be of some help. I wasn't doing a damn bit of good to anyone dressed in my fancy clothes in Paris. Eating in chic restaurants. Decorating the apartment. Hosting cocktail parties."

"You left everything behind?"

"Everything. I didn't want the money, the social position, or the luxury."

"Which is one of the reasons I admire you," he said soberly. "I've never met anyone less ambitious than you. Less acquisitive." He shook his head. "I bet your husband and his family couldn't believe what was happening."

She smiled faintly. "They couldn't. They got the best lawyers to make certain I didn't get a cent. I didn't want a cent. I agreed to everything because I just wanted out. A divorce. And freedom. I decided if I needed money, I could earn it myself."

"And after the earthquake in Turkey? What did you do then?"

"Well, by then I finally knew what I wanted to do with my life. I'd realized I have a knack for picking up languages quickly. By then I spoke French perfectly, of course, and after a really short time, I was pretty good at Turkish, too. I knew it was a talent I could use all over the world."

"You could have gone on to be a translator, found a high-paying job."

She nodded. "I could have. My parents would have liked that. But I wanted to be an aid worker. I wanted to alleviate suffering if I could. I was pretty idealistic of course: most aid workers are. You have to be."

"What did your parents say about your life?"

Felicity grimaced. "They couldn't understand why I stuck with it. They thought I'd do a little stint of charity work somewhere in the world, then come home wagging my tail, get married again and have children. Finally."

"But you never did."

"Nope. My father died twenty years ago, and I think he was sort of proud of me, even though he didn't understand my motivation. But my mother never forgave me for not giving her grandchildren, since I was their only child. She married again when she was close to eighty, adopted her new husband's children and grandchildren. So despite my being a black sheep and a disappointment, she got what she wanted, in a way."

Marek reached out and took her hand. It would have taken a superhuman effort on his part not to do so. But she touched him. Deeply. His feelings churned inside of him, chaotic, half-understood.

Her fingers curled into his, and he couldn't miss the surprise in her eyes, surprise that quickly turned to pleasure. "You always were the best hand-holder in the world," she said with a shaky grin.

He caught the tremble in her voice. "A good technique to know, hand holding." He kept his voice teasing, light, although there was anything but lightness in his heart.

"Absolutely. Like kissing." No! She was going too far now.

Her eyes twinkled. Provocative as usual. Was it an invitation? No doubt. It was also an invitation he was going to refuse. No more Felicity traps. No brief holiday affairs. Not with her, not with anyone. He forced his eyes away from the long, silver earring caught by one of her glossy curls, fought the impulse out reach out, untangle, caress. That would be a mistake, all right. Just touching her hand was something special.

"I couldn't avoid the invitation to Myra's tonight." Why was he saying this? Why did he continue? "But I'll get back to the hotel as quickly as I can, okay?"

Chapter Seven

He would much rather have been with Felicity, of course. Going out to dinner. Yet here he was, in a taxi, on his way to Myra's house. Myra. What had he and Myra ever had in common apart from their stubborn devotion to their work, their need to achieve? Even if Felicity hadn't marched into his life with her sure step, her blazing eyes, and her passion, the relationship with Myra wouldn't have continued.

Surely he and Myra wouldn't have married, would they? Impossible...wasn't it?

Perhaps not. Perhaps if he hadn't met Felicity, he would have continued on in his bland, easy way of thinking, surrounded by the same friends for years and years. Perhaps nothing would have startled him out of his torpor. Would he have conceded to a house in the suburbs and a life much like everyone else's? He didn't know. It made him uncomfortable, admitting he'd needed a Felicity in order to change the course of his entire life. If that was true, he was indebted to her for pushing him to react, to feel. To find his own strength.

He thought about Myra, remembered how she'd been in the old, days: cool, elegantly beautiful with her long, silken blonde hair falling to her waist. Beautiful, and icily self-contained. A woman who disliked body contact—not that she'd ever admitted it. But sex was something she submitted to. Myra had had only one love, one obsession: music. Nothing mattered to her as much as the beauty of Beethoven or Chopin. No one could make the sounds she needed. Only the glowing white and black keys of the piano keyboard could do that. She would play for ten, twelve hours a day.

"Are you in love with her?" Myra's face had been expressionless the day he'd first told her about Felicity. He'd felt like a traitor of course, although his relationship with Myra had begun to be perfectly platonic. Perhaps it shouldn't have started in the first place. Neither one of them had desired intensity. They hadn't had time for it. Perhaps they'd only been together out of routine, or a need to keep other people at arm's length?

"Yes. I'm in love with her."

"Fine. Good luck." Not even the faintest inflection in her voice. She'd stood up, walked to the door, hesitated. Yes, there was something she'd wanted to say. He waited, knowing it wasn't going to be gracious.

"You'll need luck." Her eyes were chips of ice. "That Felicity. She's a real bitch."

Yes, those had been her last words, all right. He remembered them now as his taxi pulled up in front of a large, elegant house, one set back from the road. Expensive. The house of people who'd done well for themselves, who belonged to the best clubs, played tennis, owned horses. People who lived very well indeed, with luxurious moderation—if such a thing could be said to exist.

The front door sprang open before his finger had time to press the bell. Myra had been looking out for him, had been anticipating his arrival. For how long? Instantly, she recognized her *faux pas*. And he saw how she tried to cover up by turning her face into a tight smiling mask. "Come in, Marek. Come in. Sam will be a little delayed. There's a big law suit pending."

"Fine. Now we'll have time to catch up on things. This is a lovely house, Myra." It was; he wasn't lying. It was airy, light, and spacious.

Myra led him through a long hall hung with tasteful watercolors and into a flawlessly decorated living room. Yes, this was the sort of setting he'd pictured Myra in. It was what she'd always wanted, even back then, in the old hippie days, when everyone had insisted on simplicity, on rejection of the consumer society. It was also the sort of setting he found suffocating. Then. And now. No, he'd never have been able to give Myra something like this.

"Whiskey? I'm about to pour one for myself."

"Yes, fine." Surprised, he didn't show it. Myra struck him as the last person to drink whiskey. She'd hated alcohol, had avoided it at all costs—although why he still remembered that too, he didn't know. She must even be less comfortable than he imagined; he noted her tight face, the tension in her movements.

"Of course you'll have to meet my grandchildren. Two of them are here, visiting for a few days." Myra handed him a glass, and they both sat down on a luxurious white sofa.

"Grandchildren! How time flies." *Here we go*, Marek thought wryly. *The small talk has begun.* Of course, this was why he'd been invited. She wanted to show him how, in her way, she'd succeeded. She lived in this big house, was married, had a family. She was still chic, elegant, and almost self-assured. She hadn't needed him, Marek, to get what she'd wanted in life.

"Yes. We have three sons, Ross, Kenny, and Warren. Ross and Kenny are married and have three children each. And you? Did you marry? Do you have children? You see, I know nothing about your private life although there's always an article in one magazine or another about your philosophy in life and your work."

"I try to keep my private life just that. Private. But yes. I was married, then divorced several short years later." It wasn't something he cared to discuss now either. Not with Myra. Not here. "I have one son."

He looked around the room and searched for a change of subject. The modern expensive furniture had been cleverly combined with elegant antique tables, chairs; a very large contemporary painting hung on one wall; and huge picture windows gave out onto a garden with perfect flowers and a flawless stretch of lawn. There was one element missing, however. Something important, something he couldn't overlook.

"There's no piano." He raised his eyebrows and looked at Myra quizzically. Was he wrong or did she flush slightly?

"No," she answered quickly—too quickly, nervously and almost defiantly. "There's a piano up in the music room, but I'm afraid my boys never showed much interest in that object." She made a face. "And my grandchildren! They're even worse. If it isn't electronic and very noisy, music just doesn't seem to count these days."

"But what about you?" His voice was soft. "What about your passion for music?"

"Oh that!" She shrugged, forced out a little laugh meant to illustrate how unimportant, how banal, her old dream had been. "My passion for playing music developed into a passion for listening to it a long time ago. We have an excellent symphony orchestra here in San Francisco, you know. And so many chamber groups."

"But you didn't continue?"

"No. I didn't continue." She didn't meet his eyes. "I carried on playing after my marriage, but when the children came, I let myself drift into a life of leisure." The tight, tense smile was dismissive. "I discovered my real vocation was looking after my home and family. Besides, there are all the charities. They take up an enormous amount of my time. If women like me don't devote ourselves to such things, nothing would ever get done, you know."

"You don't have to justify your life, Myra. I'm certain the work you do is very necessary."

"We all have to compromise, don't we? I don't think I was concert pianist material anyway."

Did she really believe that? She'd been good, very good. Brilliant? He wasn't certain. Still, she shouldn't have given up. But he wanted to be soothing. Not for him to tell her she'd perhaps made a terrible mistake. "Of course we have to compromise. Age usually lends us wisdom."

Her expression became scornful. "I should hope so. We were so idealistic back then. Too idealistic. Silly even." She sneered at their youth.

"Idealism isn't silly, Myra. I think it's admirable."

"Do you?" The smile on her mouth turned bitter. "How about that Felicity Powers? How far has her idealism gotten her these days? You saw what she looked like!" Myra wrinkled her nose.

I did indeed. She looked wonderful.

"She looked like a dried-up hayseed, that's what! You'd think she's never heard about makeup! All that horrible long white hair. Shameful. It makes her look like an ancient crone. Why doesn't she cut it, dye it? Do something decent with it. And those awful clothes she wore! Rags from a junk shop."

Certainly not Yves Saint Laurent. That would be hard to imagine, thought Marek, amused.

"She said something last night about having helped on foreign aid projects," Myra continued spitefully. "How she'd once delivered ink and paper to a war zone or some other madness. I've never heard something so silly! Think of all the refugees living in camps, hungry and cold. And she leads a convoy of ink into a Serbian war zone?"

Felicity was right. Myra hated her.

"As she explained, the best way to bring down a government is to work from the inside. The ink and the paper were being transported to the opposition so they could continue to publish information about what was really going on."

"I suppose one can always justify anything." It wasn't a question. It was a challenge, an attack, and a conclusion.

But he wasn't here to discuss Felicity Powers. Certainly not with Myra. The situation was almost comic. Almost. Myra, was finally making the long-awaited scene of jealousy—some forty-three years too late. "Does one have to justify?" he asked quietly. "We all do what we think is right in a given situation."

"Of course." Myra's smile was bitter. Scathing. "I'm all right. You're all right. Everyone's just fine and dandy. That's how things went in the old days, didn't they? I love you, you love me, and good-bye. We all said we loved everybody, and of course we didn't. We were just young puppies playing around. Thank goodness there's more sanity in our children nowadays. My boys were never as foolish as we were."

Was there really sanity now and only madness then? In any case, he wouldn't question what she'd said. Myra needed to believe her own children were sane, calm, and protected. But Marek hoped they weren't: everyone needs a little madness, a little freedom. Perhaps they'd been wise enough to hide their youthful madness from their mother?

Before he could think of a suitable reply, something to ease the strain, Sam made his entrance. Marek was so relieved, he could have jumped up and kissed the man.

"Sorry for the delay," Sam's voice boomed heartily. His eyes took in the two of them, assessed the tension. Correctly sensing his wife's trouble, he immediately went over to Myra and put his arm around her shoulders, protectively. "Has Marek met the boys yet?"

"There hasn't really been a chance..."

"Our grandson, Keith, was in seventh heaven when I told him you'd be here," said Sam turning to Marek. "He dreams of being a writer. Perhaps you could give him a few tips. He wants to specialize in science fiction."

"Of course," said Marek hoping the painful resignation didn't show too clearly on his face. It was definitely going to be a long, long evening.

****

She wasn't here. There was her tatty bag, over there on the floor, in the corner of the hotel room where she'd left it last night. But the room was empty, the air still. A perfectly empty room, as though Felicity had never really been here. There wasn't even the faint whiff of her perfume—a subtle perfume, uniquely hers, one that had never come out of a bottle.

Not a note from her telling him where she was, not here, not down at reception. The soft light of the lamp on the desk touched the emptiness with sad and subtle shadow. There was a stray hairpin beside the paper cup vase with its one red rose. Madness. That's what that gesture had been. Bringing Felicity a rose.

She was out somewhere. Where? He could almost picture her. Hair flying in the usual disorder as she tipped her head back to laugh. In a bar somewhere? In the middle of a crowd, men all around her. Amused men's faces. She always amused, always had been the center of attention. And yes, she did need to win approval from all and sundry—she hadn't exaggerated when she'd said that.

He realized how angry he was. He fought against the feeling of betrayal. But had she betrayed him? Of course not. He'd betrayed himself. Didn't want to get involved with her? Is that what he'd told himself? Fool.

All evening there had been just one image in his mind, one person in his head. His heart had beat wildly with anticipation. Guiltily, not as subtly as he should have, he'd managed to concoct excuses for a hasty departure from Myra's. Now, here he was. In the room. Alone.

It wasn't the fact he was alone that bothered him, was it? But he'd been here before. Once. A long time ago.

****

"Laundry? You want me to do laundry?" Felicity's voice had risen, had taken on a high tremolo of warning. "What kind of macho trip are we on here, Sumner!"

He forced himself to stay calm, as usual. "I merely suggested—get this, Felicity—*suggested* you have more free time than I do. And since I am rather backlogged at the moment—or should I say *smothered* in paperwork—you could use some of your free time to do the laundry."

"Yeah. Right. I've got it. *Boy*, have I got it. We live together for nine months, right? And for nine months it's all kootchie-koo." Her voice took on a mimicking tone. "Oh, Felicity, dear. I really do respect women's rights. Really I do. I don't want some bag dragging about the house in slippers and a nightgown, at my beck and call for a pot roast and a squeeze in the night. No. I want independence in a woman. I want a woman who knows what she wants and goes for it."

"Exactly. I just—"

"You just! You bet you just. You just gave me orders to go out and do laundry. For nine months we go out, do laundry together. Hand in hand, all the way to the laundromat. A coffee, an ice cream while the dryer's going. Cute as they come, right? Then bingo! Today the scales fall from my eyes. Today begins the new era. The era of domesticity."

"Look, can we just forget I asked the favor? Can we now ignore this minor domestic incident? Pretend I never said a word about not having a clean sock, or a pair of underpants to slap onto my body. And I have to go out to work teaching, for crying out loud, as well as writing this damned thesis. And you come floating in, laughing about how you spent all morning in some fern bar talking with Jenny and Libbet and Margie about women's rights."

"Right! Just drop it. Just like that!" Her eyes blazed. Her red hair seemed to glow like a fire. He loved her and he hated her at the same time.

"Yeah. Right on. Just like that."

"And tomorrow? What happens tomorrow?" She wasn't going to drop anything. When Felicity went into battle she did it in full regalia. No wishy-washy words like concession and defeat in her vocabulary.

"Tomorrow?" Marek closed his eyes with fatigue, infinite patience.

"Yeah. Tomorrow. Tomorrow promises to be full of surprises. If I'm lucky, it's bound to have ironing in it. And stew? And dishes to wash. And a baby."

"A baby?" There was a quick furl of panic in his gut. Was it panic? Or...

"I can see it all now, Sumner. The vision is rolling itself out before my very eyes. I can hear you saying the words, really I can."

"What words, damn it?" He was losing his cool.

She sneered, her hard lips curling maliciously at the corners. "Oh Felicity, how nice you would look pregnant. With my little one in your belly. My son."

"For God's sake, Felicity!" What else would she bring up? The worst of it was, he did think she would look beautiful pregnant. He did like the idea of their child growing in her belly. What the hell was wrong with that? Thank goodness, he'd never brought the subject up. Thank goodness he'd never said a word.

Thank goodness. Because now, as of this moment, things were perfectly clear.

"Get this straight, Sumner. No babies, right? No baby diapers, no bottles, no happy families. Life is big—or it can be. I'm not going to spend my years shoving a stroller through a rotten suburban shopping center. If that's what you want, a breeder, go back to My-rah."

Those words had been the parting shot. The last bullet fired. She'd flounced out into the afternoon then, the door slam a nuclear crack behind her.

He'd spent the rest of the day writing—or trying to. By six he was out in the street, buying food, a bottle of red wine, candles. By seven the dinner was prepared—exactly what she loved, little delicacies: sushi, mushrooms in soya sauce.

Then came the long evening of waiting. The candles were there on the table, the places set. Ten o'clock. Eleven. Twelve.

He felt betrayed—by his own foolishness as much as by Felicity. Candles, indeed. Where the hell was she! Was she coming back? What if she never came back? What if it was over? Did he mind? Oh yes, he minded all right. He loved her. More than was decently possible.

At one thirty in the morning, she made her entrance.

He'd been sitting in the armchair over by the window, re-reading what he'd written that afternoon (pure unadulterated, garbled rubbish).

Her eyes were glowing; loose copper tendrils of hair flowed around her face.

"You'll never believe what I've been up to!" She

dumped a huge stuffed pillowcase on the sofa. Her anger, the battle earlier that day, had already been forgotten.

"No. I probably won't."

She stopped still. "You probably won't what?"

"Believe what you've been up to."

"What's that supposed to mean?" She frowned, jabbed a finger into the softness of the pillowcase. "Hey, wait a minute, Marek. You know what that is?"

"Go on." He was icy.

"Laundry, that's what. I've done the laundry."

"Laundry? You didn't walk out the door with laundry, as I recall."

"No. I didn't. I walked out the door hating your guts. And then I came back in to apologize—at six fifteen. And you were gone. So I got all the dirty clothes together and went out and did my duty. As a female." Her voice was heavily laced with sarcasm, but he could see she wasn't angry. Miffed, perhaps, but definitely conciliatory.

"Go on."

"Go on?"

"That's right. You left at six fifteen with the laundry, and it took you until one thirty in the morning to work out how to put the money in the machine."

"Right. Stupid old Felicity Powers. Needs a man like Marek with her at all times."

"You know what I'm getting at."

"You betcha. You're trying to tell me I belong to you, and I should be here at your beck and call. Not out with Jenny having a good time—*after* doing the laundry."

Where had she been? Out with Jenny, in Jenny's

old car, driving out to Palo Alto to see a lover of Jenny's. A gypsy. Then, somewhere around Redwood City they'd gotten lost. "We ended up in this weird farmhouse out in the middle of nowhere where someone had been slaughtering chickens. Marek, imagine! They'd strung all those chickens up on the branches of trees! We caught sight of them in the car headlights! It was ghastly!"

Then she'd suddenly stopped talking because she'd seen the candles, the plates, the cutlery, and utter dismay crossed her face.

"Oh Marek. How could I have known?" Her shoulders sagged with sudden defeat; her face lost its color. "I'm sorry. I'm so sorry. I should have called." She made a helpless gesture. Crossed the room and threw herself into his arms.

"I love you so much Marek. I love you, I love you, I love you. I don't want to quarrel with you. I hate the way it feels. It's just—oh, sometimes I can't stop myself. It just wells up in me, the anger. And then it's too late."

Old memories of old arguments. Old feelings of being abandoned.

And now, tonight, new ones.

He'd wanted to see her sitting over there on the bed, when he'd walked in the door from the tedious dinner at Myra's. He'd wanted to see her, head tilted toward him, the dark fire of her eyes showing him he mattered. He knew he did—or at least he thought he did. It had been there, that look, that want, that need. All morning he'd seen it, and all day, as they'd crossed the city, the heat of the pavement shivering under their feet.

"Until later," she'd said. Her voice had been soft. He hadn't given a return sign. His eyes hadn't betrayed him. He hadn't wanted her to know her words were important to him.

"Until later," he'd answered and kept his voice cool, unresponsive. No promises.

Her eyes had flickered briefly. Confusion? Then the expression, fleeting, instantaneous, was gone.

Where the hell was she?

His need caught him up short.

Now what? Was he going to wait here, a patsy, a prey to these almost unbearable emotions? Waiting for Felicity? No, he wasn't. Not that. Anything but that.

He was heading down the coast, he'd said to Myra and Sam at the Bookworm last night. He wasn't staying here in San Francisco. He had a past to conjure up—his own past. This was a pilgrimage of his own making. Felicity had been a part of it. Now she was somewhere else, and he'd better get out while the going was good. Get out before the warm, deep waters engulfed him.

He slapped open his dark brown leather valise and began throwing his clothes into it. He'd leave her a note, brief, polite. Write about how nice it had been to see her again after all these years. About how sweet— yes, that was the word—how *sweet* it had been for her to look him up. There were things he had to do, places he had to go to. Alone.

She could stay here in the room as long as she liked—at his expense, of course. He'd arrange for the bill to be paid.

Enough was enough.

He was certain she didn't have his address. She wouldn't come after him. Not Felicity. Not again.

Chapter Eight

"Making a quick getaway?" Felicity stood in the doorway taking in the scene: the open but fully packed suitcase on the bed, Marek's trench coat flung over the table. He was on his way out. No denying the evidence.

Marek sat in the armchair by the window, his face tight, his eyes haunted. "I'm sitting here, in a chair, right? Aren't the words 'a quick getaway' somewhat of an exaggeration?" He drawled the words out slowly, mockingly.

"Okay then. A slow getaway."

He stared at her, unable to pull his eyes away. Her face was pale, her expression wild. Loose tendrils of hair shadowed her neck, calling attention to the slow throb of veins under the delicate skin. She looked sexy as hell. Tempting and far too dangerous to think about.

"Not quick, not slow. Neither one of the above. No getaway." His voice was icy, impersonal.

"That!" Her arm waved wildly, gesticulated in the direction of the suitcase. A sharp, searing feeling of betrayal mixed with humiliation kept her tense, unrelenting. "I mean, if you want me out of here, all you have to do is tell me. Since you're obviously desperate to get rid of me." She felt as if she'd been stabbed. She crossed the room slowly until she was standing beside him, staring down at him, her eyes flashing with determination and fury. "But let's not forget you were the one who invited me up here. Remember? I didn't ask to be put up in your hotel room."

But you might have done so. If he hadn't taken matters into his own hands. Well, never again. Never. *Your time is up as far as I'm concerned, Marek Sumner!*

He stood, studied her for a minute.

"God, you're beautiful." It was as if the words had been wrenched out of him, as if he'd have given anything not to have said them. But they made her heart stand still.

She wasn't going to let herself be flattered. Flattery! Why, it was the oldest trick in the book! She wasn't going to let herself melt. Yet she did. She tried not to relent. She tried not to feel triumphant. Intuitively, she saw—or felt—the beginning of a capitulation, the raw need in him. Her anger vanished into the warm, soft air of the California night.

He was losing the battle. Thank goodness, he was losing. She would be his lover. They would drift away together on the deep river of sensation. She could almost feel his skin on hers, feel the muscles bunching in his back, in his shoulders as she arched into him.

She shook her head violently. *Letting desire ruin your reason!* Because he wasn't moving toward her. His hands weren't reaching out to stroke, to caress, to love her. It was just the opposite. He'd wanted to avoid her, and she'd have a hell of a job winning him over.

"I'm beautiful?" There was the edge of bitterness she couldn't keep out of her voice. "Is that why you're running away?"

"I'm not running anywhere. I was waiting for you.

Despite my better instincts. Despite my impulse to leave you here, get out as fast as I can." Words of passion, but not the words she really wanted to hear.

She stared, not knowing what to do, how to reach him. His green eyes were dark, cold, un-giving, his mouth a tight line. "What's that supposed to mean?" She was determined not to let herself soften.

"Come on. We're leaving."

"Leaving where?" She stepped back warily.

"San Francisco. I've ordered a car."

"It's midnight." As if that had anything to do with it.

Marek strode quickly over to the bed, snapped his leather case shut. Reached down, scooped up Felicity's bag, and headed out into the hall.

She grabbed the red rose in its cup, almost had to run in order to keep up with him. "Don't bother asking me if *I* want to go with you," she called after him as she stepped through the doorway. "Don't ask *my* opinion about anything!" But he didn't have to. She'd go, all right.

The rented car was waiting for them in front of the hotel. Marek tossed the bags into the trunk, slipped behind the wheel, started the engine, and headed out of the city. Felicity wondered what the urgency was. Where were they going? Marek turned left on the old coast road. Why this trip in the night? *Unless he wants to avoid spending the night with me, in the same bed.* The idea depressed her, and she preferred not to dwell on it.

"We're going south?"

"Right."

"Downright communicative, the man is. Los

Angeles? Mexico? Go on. Tell me you've got Brazil in mind."

"Argentina," he said drily.

The road was empty. She could just make out the long, flat line of slumbering ocean on her right. Places they'd been to long ago. Could she even recognize them? Yes, some of them. This place, for instance. Right across from the strip of beach, here where the city had once come to a straggling end, just before the start of suburban towns and low, scrubby mountains.

"Hey, Marek! I know where we are now. There on the left, that's where the really bad rock concert took place! Do you remember? The concert for the student benefit fund."

"Vaguely."

"Where I met the vampire."

"What vampire?"

"Don't tell me you've forgotten?" She forced a note of mock disappointment into her voice.

Marek's brow furrowed with the effort of remembering. No, he couldn't remember anything about a vampire. "Sorry. I really have forgotten."

"Well, I certainly haven't. He was horrible." Felicity screwed up her face in disgust. "Of course, you weren't the one he talked to."

"No. You're the social butterfly. The one who ends up having impossible conversations with every strange or unsavory person who crosses your path."

"That's what being an extrovert is all about."

"All right. Go on. Tell me about the vampire."

"It was during one of the breaks at the concert. You were off somewhere else in the room, deep in heavy intellectual literary conversation, no doubt."

"No doubt."

"And he came up to me. He gave me the creeping willies right from the start."

"The creeping willies? Do the scars still show?"

She pretended to ignore him, but it was impossible to miss the softened expression on his face. "I remember that vampire as clearly as if the meeting happened yesterday. A horrible man with stringy, black greasy hair. A dirty-looking beard. And mad eyes. Gruesome! Just what you don't want to meet in a dark alley."

"And you decided he was a vampire." The corners of his mouth twitched up into a faint smile.

If only she could make him laugh! If only she could make defiance disappear from his eyes, then everything would be all right.

"I didn't decide anything! Marek. He came up to me and *told* me he was a vampire. Said he roamed the streets during the full moon looking for stray cats and dogs whose blood he could drink. That he didn't know how long he'd be able to hold off for before starting to attack people."

"Fact or fantasy?"

"He kept staring at my neck in the most horrible way."

"Your beautiful long neck." The smile was broadening. "Even I'm getting ideas now."

"You don't look at my neck in a horrible way," she provoked. "Even if you did, I don't think I'd mind. On the contrary."

The look he shot her was inscrutable...almost. And interested? Excited?

"I know that." His voice was quiet.

"A fact as big as the nose on my face, huh? I suppose where you're concerned, I just can't help making a fool of myself." She took a deep breath. "Marek? Are you trying to make it perfectly clear you don't want me? Is that why you rushed me out of the hotel room?"

"That's our Felicity. Come straight to the heart of the matter. No beating around the bush."

"And that's no answer."

"No. It's not. It's an appreciation." His voice was dry.

She waited, watched as his fingers tightened on the steering wheel. "You do want me, don't you." A statement, not a question.

"All right. I want you. Fine. And then what? What are you looking for? A quick screw for old time's sake?"

"That's our Marek! Smooth-sounding. Romantic. Seductive. Always a man with a gift for the gab." How could he know what would happen between the two of them? She couldn't say something so obvious, though. It would sound too much like begging.

"We come from two different worlds. Two different planets."

"Two different galaxies, even. With serious communication problems." She forced herself to laugh to keep from crying, but the sound wasn't convincing.

For the first time there was compassion in his face. He reached over, squeezed her hand. "Look, how about if we just enjoy each other's company for a while. Like friends. Good, old friends. Okay?"

"I feel like the family dog." She sniffed. "Begging for scraps. Woof, woof!"

"More like the family hyena."

"Is that a compliment, too?"

"Time for a change of subject. Look, Felicity. Over there, on the right. Do you remember this place?"

She peered into the night. "No. Where are we?"

"Half Moon Bay. The nudist beach."

"Goodness. I forgot about that. All the horrible men who stood at the top of the cliff with binoculars, staring down!"

"A sight worth seeing." He leered.

"I certainly wasn't." She sighed. "I looked like a pale white string bean splotched with thousands of freckles."

"Not exactly the image my memory conjures up."

"And I thought we shared all the same ones. Hey, Marek…do you think this is the right sort of conversation to have with the family-dog-cum-hyena?"

"Long, slinky, lanky. You still are."

"A lean cur."

"A sleek, elegant greyhound." He chuckled. "With a hyena mind."

"Watch your step, Sumner. You might be fooling yourself. You sound interested. Very interested."

High above, the night sky was amazing clear. Diamond stars winked cheerfully, and the moon sent a shiver of light across an ink sea. It was good being here. Why complain? *Take what's coming your way and take it with good grace*, she told herself.

"Look, Felicity. There's another landmark. Remember?"

She could just make out the steady yellow light glowing on the horizon. "Right! That twenty-four hour café! Ye Olde Greasye Spoone, we called it!"

"And forke. And knifee. With the best Spanish omelets this side of the equator."

"Greasy Spanish omelets."

"Are you hungry?"

She wasn't. She didn't think she could eat a thing. "Didn't Myra feed you any dinner?"

"She did. Very refined. Too much so. I feel a need for the prosaic."

"I suppose Myra also said terrible things about me?" She felt wary. Very wary. Did she really want to know what Myra had told him?

"Not terrible things. She just wanted to point out your world is different from hers and mine."

"What do you think?"

"It is." He nodded, pulled the car off the road and into the gravel-covered parking lot of the café. "But, on the other hand, her world isn't my world either."

"Does my world scare you?"

"Should it?"

"No. It should intrigue you. It should make you want to try it out."

He turned off the engine, stared ahead into the night. "Meaning what?"

"Meaning, come with me. Let me show you places. A field of flowers in the middle of Flanders. A bleak mountain in Turkey, beige with dust and beautiful against a perfectly blue sky. The Sahara at night with a million stars overhead. The Negev and its ruined, forgotten ancient cities." Her voice held the promise of boundless horizons.

Did he want those horizons? Did he need them? He opened the car door, stepped out into the cool, salty night. What did he have to lose? He stopped the longing before it carried him away. *What do you have to gain?*

The diner hadn't changed much since the seventies. Yellow walls, a long, Formica counter. Cheap metal-legged tables, plastic chairs. A heavy odor of fried-out fat hung on the air. Aside from a chunky, bored-looking cook in a dirty white apron who stood picking at his teeth with a frazzled toothpick, the place was empty.

"Damn flies," muttered the cook. "No room for people anymore there's so many flies."

"Flies?" Felicity looked around her. This might indeed be the perfect haven for flies, but there weren't any, aside from a few unlucky victims caught miserably on a curl of yellow flypaper suspended above a prehistoric cash register.

"Damn flies everywhere you look."

Not even a buzz stirred the greasy air. Felicity threw Marek a look of complicity. A nut. California was full of them. As if the odds and ends of humanity all rolled over to the west coast and stopped there, the ocean forbidding further movement.

"You still do Spanish omelets?"

The cook shifted his hostile little eyes suspiciously in their direction. "If the damn flies let me get any work done."

"Right," encouraged Marek. He led Felicity in the direction of a corner booth. "Two Spanish omelets."

"Without flies," added Felicity. "If possible, that is. I'm a fervent vegetarian." She heard Marek's muffled guffaw.

"You aren't really, are you?" he asked after a minute.

"I'm off flies at the moment."

"Right. Two Spanish omelets without flies."

124

Marek's eyes glowed. "I think I'm going to like being a vegetarian, too."

Egg shells cracked against a razor-sharp spatula. Butter hissed on the hot surface of the grill plate.

"I guess I'm hungry after all." Felicity sighed. She was. "No. I'll correct that. I'm absolutely ravenous."

"What did you have for dinner?"

"I didn't. No My-rahs are out there begging for my company." She stopped, looked slightly ashamed of herself. "Meow." Then she snickered. "Good heavens. I'm almost a whole zoo."

"If Myra doesn't invite you to dinner, you don't eat?" He was mocking her.

"I just felt like walking. And thinking."

"That's where you were? Out walking? And thinking?"

"That's where I was." She eyed him curiously. "Where did you think I was?"

He remembered how jealous he'd felt, how he'd pictured her in some bar charming the daylights out of an admiring crowd. "I didn't."

"Liar." A light bulb clicked on in her head. "Come on, Marek. Tell me what you were thinking. Is that why you packed up your bags? Because you thought I should be sitting there in the hotel room? Waiting for you?"

Yes. "Don't get carried away, Felicity. Your imagination is working overtime." He tried to look innocent. And failed.

"Down, Rover! Woof. The family dog shouldn't think."

"I didn't put you in the family dog category. You put yourself there."

"The good old trusty friend. That's what you said."

He sighed. "Okay. What else do you want to hear? That you are infinitely desirable? Beautiful? A pleasure to my eyes?"

"Sounds good. We're making progress." She stared, took a deep breath. "Now tell me if you mean that…what you just said."

He hesitated only for a second before relenting. "I meant it."

"Wow." She slumped back in her seat, stared at him with unbelieving eyes.

"Here's them omelets. You folks want something to drink?"

"Felicity?" Marek watched her curiously.

She fought her way back through a haze of emotion. "Uh, um, oh yes. A beer. A beer would be fine."

"Two beers. Without flies," Marek said firmly.

"Can't guarantee nothing without flies," said the cook threateningly. "Damn flies get in everywheres."

"Eat your omelet," Marek ordered her. "It'll taste terrible when it's cold."

"Won't taste like much hot either. My appetite just disappeared again." Still, she had to make an effort. The wonderful odor of tomatoes, peppers, and cumin floated up, tickled her nose temptingly.

"No place like California for flies." Two frosty glasses of beer appeared on the table. "Life's not worth nothing in this damn state if you ain't a damn fly."

"I don't see any flies. Honestly I don't." Felicity pronged the egg.

"I'll just bet you don't," said the cook sulkily. "Damn things go all invisible. Camouflage themselves

126

like lizards. You look at a piece of wall and that ain't wall you're seeing."

"It's a damn fly," she encouraged.

"Damn right it's a damn fly." He moved off.

"Things could be worse," said Marek laconically. "Could be something bigger. Like pigeons. Pigeons all over the walls."

"Or pterodactyls," Felicity added. "Think about it. They're huge! They'd make a real mess of the place. Think of the size of sticky pterodactyl paper you'd have to order!"

"Hard to hide a pterodactyl in an omelet, though." Marek was laughing.

"Who knows? What if it's in camouflage? Hey, Marek? Guess what. Flies or no flies, this omelet tastes glorious."

****

"Do you want to tell me what this excursion is all about now? Like, where we're going, for example? Or is it still top secret?"

They were back in the car, heading down the coast again. Perhaps she shouldn't have asked. For a minute she even thought he wouldn't answer her. She watched his profile, etched against the night: tight, tense, and remarkably beautiful. "Marek?" Her fingers reached out, touched his arm. She needed the contact. "Come back from wherever you are."

He sighed. "Part of the pilgrimage. Yet another vista in the voyage down memory lane."

"Which vista are we doing?"

"Island Park."

"Oh." Her eyes searched his face for some semblance of warmth, but it had gone again. Island

Park. The place where Marek had grown up. She'd been there before. And the experience had been disastrous. Another disaster on the long list of things gone wrong between them.

She hadn't been sufficiently equipped for that detour into Marek's past. For the reality. Not back then. What a terrible snob she must have been! Despite the thin veneer of easy living in the Haight, the oft repeated, verbal refusal of material comfort, her rejection of her father's offer of increased financial assistance.

That awful place! Island Park! How well she remembered the cheap scramble of wooden houses strung out along a shabby beach of dirty-looking sand. *Her* Marek couldn't have come from such tawdriness! He couldn't. Not the self-assured, wonderful Marek who strode through the Haight with such assurance and grace. But he had.

She'd always known there was an enormous difference in their backgrounds. She'd been so protected, growing up in the elegance of well-off New York society, a world of opera, and concerts, private school, and ease. A world where no one raised a voice. A world at once polite and respectful. He'd mentioned his family from time to time too, hinted at the poverty, the shoddiness of his background. But had given her no details.

He hadn't wanted her with him either. Not at first. He had to go home for the weekend, he'd said. To see his mother, see if she was okay: he was all she had.

"She has your father too, right?"

"A real present, he is. A shining example of the human race." His voice had been flat and expressionless.

"What's that supposed to mean?"

He told her. Finally. About the alcohol. The violence he'd been subjected to as a child. That his mother was subjected to still.

"But it's horrible," Felicity had protested. "Why does your mother stay with him?" Such martyrdom lay outside of her frame of reference.

"Because women like my mother don't believe in divorce. She's from Poland and extremely religious. A wife's duty is to cope as best as she can. The rewards come later. In heaven."

"How utterly backward."

They had driven down the coast in a rattling old car borrowed from a friend, stopping every few miles to cool the engine and make minor repairs. The afternoon had been hot. Marek had shrugged off his T-shirt, opened the hood, battled with a reluctant carburetor. Felicity had sat on the grassy roadside, watching him as he worked, watching the faint beads of sweat pearling along his tight biceps, noting the play of muscles down his back. He was a sight well worth watching. Magnificent, was the word in her mind. A magnificent man in his prime.

"You think there's any chance of this car really getting us there?"

It had. Finally…unfortunately.

"Home sweet home," Marek had announced as they pulled off the main road, joined a dirt track leading toward a scruffy little bay.

His parents lived in the third house. Once it had been gray. Once. A long time before. Now any remaining paint was scaled and curled. Sagging wooden steps led up to a tattered screen door tapping with sullen repetition in the relentless sea breeze. Inside, there had been a worn, sticky-feeling oilcloth on the cheap square table. The walls were damp and moldy; a television blared. The sickening smell of boiled fish was imbedded in the ragged curtains, in the lumpy cloth of a defeated sofa.

Tacky. *What am I doing here?* Felicity tried to hide her repulsion. Why had she insisted Marek bring her here? Why had she pushed so hard? She could have done without this vision. The tawdry aspects of Marek's life would never hold any fascination for her. Especially if the tawdriness threatened to nibble away at the sparkling image of Marek, her beautiful lover.

She'd been such a young fool, thinking you could close your eyes to reality.

Marek's father had barely looked up when they entered. He was a sloppy, ruined droop of a man, clothed in a sagging undershirt and greasy looking trousers. Impossible to miss the cruel mockery in his eyes when he'd caught sight of Marek.

"Well, well. Mister University paying the poor folks at home a visit." His voice was a grunted sneer. He hated his son, Felicity could see that immediately.

Horrified, she'd searched the man's face. Where was the resemblance to his son? Where was the refined beauty, the sculptured lines of the jaw, the deep set of his green eyes? Surely such a brute could never have fathered a son with such fine features, such an acute intelligence!

Marek's mother, pale, nondescript, watched her son with adoring eyes. Fearful eyes. As if terrified he'd vanish at any second. The meal had been intolerable, the conversation strained.

"Mrs. Kennedy over at Butterworth told me to send her greetings. Her son Pat works over at the slaughter yard now."

"Doing a decent job instead of stuffing his head with garbage," grunted Marek's father. This, from a man who'd given up any thought of work years before.

Marek's mother had watched Felicity covertly out of the corner of her eye. Without warmth. Felicity had still forced herself to smile politely, although she positively itched to get away from here, from the odors, the hint of barely suppressed violence. What could she say to these people? But kindly, well-brought up, she'd scrabbled about in her mind for any subject that would permit correct conversation.

"Those are such lovely wildflowers outside! So colorful."

The older woman refused Felicity's attempts, and she felt foolish. And like an impostor: Lady Bountiful visiting the poor cottagers. And the cottagers could see right through the façade, could feel her condescension. She hated herself at that moment. She hated being here. She hated being in this position. She wanted out!

Marek's mother had cried when they left, dabbing at the tears with the corner of her apron.

Neither she nor Marek had ever talked about the visit. A disaster.

She'd make it up to him, Felicity thought. She'd show him what a real family was all about. She invited him to New York to meet her parents.

"I'm not doing it so you can see the contrast in our backgrounds. I just want to show you the word 'family' does have other possibilities." Marek was worth more than the belittlement of his father. Her family would accept him, she knew. They would be kind, encouraging, warm. Simply because she, the darling daughter, had brought him home. And her family was—well—the opposite to his! Night and day, summer and winter, hatred and acceptance. Felicity might well be a rebel, but her parents took her protest with ease and indulgence. They loved their daughter; they were liberal.

She remembered the hard set to Marek's jaw, the closed expression in his eyes as soon as he entered the 72nd street townhouse. Then there had been tea and biscuits at the elegant, antique table in the sitting room.

"Felicity tells us you're doing your doctorate on Thomas Hardy?"

When he'd deigned to answer, it had been through stiff lips.

Marek had exploded when later, leaving her parents behind, Felicity and he walked through the frigid winter streets of New York. Walked? He strode with determined, angry steps, knowing full well he was going too fast for her, and not caring if he was. A harsh wind lashed her cheeks as she stumbled in her attempt to keep up with him.

"They want to make certain the man their daughter is with will be a good earner. I'm being judged as a potential respectable husband. When our little rebellion is finished, that is. When we've finally decided to give in and become normal citizens."

"Marek! I can't help the kind of family I come from any more than you can! Just because they're relatively wealthy and I've been brought up comfortably doesn't mean I subscribe to my parent's values!"

"Doesn't it? Then why bring me here? Why insist I meet your family?"

"Because my family is part of me just like yours is part of you," she'd moaned miserably. "Marek! Stop this! Stop walking so quickly and listen to me."

"I *am* listening to you. Can't you see that? I'm listening and observing."

"How incredibly patronizing of you!"

"And I see exactly the kind of person you'll become in a few years time. You'll be exactly like your mother. Oh, it's not a criticism." He held up his hands in protest. "There's nothing wrong with your mother. She's nice, and kind, and polite, and refined. And intelligent enough to see if she allows her daughter enough leeway now, dear Felicity will eventually knuckle down, be the sort of society matron she was raised to be."

She'd stopped dead. Stopped rushing after him. What was the point of trying to convince him he'd gotten everything all wrong? "Bastard!" she'd spit out after him.

He'd turned. "Does the truth hurt?" He was almost sneering.

She'd forced herself to be calm. "Because it *isn't* the truth, it can't possibly hurt. What does hurt..." She'd taken a deep breath. "What does hurt me, is how bitter you are. How resentful. Because you never had the advantages I've had. And you hate me for it. And because you don't trust me to hold to my convictions. *That* hurts."

It had been their worst argument. They had never talked about it either. Never. Indeed, their relationship had barely survived it. Two days later, they'd taken the bus back to San Francisco—after Marek had stiffly refused to let Felicity's father pay for plane fare. Felicity had winced with misery. Her father couldn't have known how badly Marek would take such an offer.

Back in San Francisco, back in the Haight, the easy atmosphere had helped hide the wounds. Street music, smiles, talk of revolution. Felicity no longer dared meet Marek's eyes when the talk veered around to the evils of the bourgeois society. She didn't want to see his mockery. She didn't want to have to hate him because he didn't believe in her.

Now, in the end, all these long years later, she knew she'd proved him wrong. Her life had been totally different from the one he'd thought her programmed for. It was a triumph, of sorts, but it didn't make her happier knowing she'd won. Not at the moment. Not here on the coast road, heading back to Island Park.

"Marek?"

He glanced at her briefly, his eyes dark.

"Do your parents still live in Island Park?"

"My mother died twenty-seven years ago." His voice was flat, emotionless.

"I'm sorry." She paused. "And your father? What about him?" She wanted to tell herself to stop prying, but still, she wanted to know. Had to know.

"He disappeared. Went off with another woman five days after my mother's death. I never heard another word either from or about him."

"You're a lucky man, then." Oh help. Why couldn't she just keep her big mouth shut!

To her surprise he turned, laughed. "Don't I know

it."

****

Once, he could have made his way back here blindfolded. He hadn't needed to check signposts or count turnoffs along the twisting coast road. It was a flat countryside, with no visible accentuation. Artichoke fields followed other artichoke fields, gave way, finally, to the military lines of Brussels sprouts before coming back to artichokes. The high cliffs had long vanished, and long grasses waved bleakly before disappearing into the occasional dark redwood forest.

They arrived in Island Park just as the black sky was easing its way into early morning's deep, marine blue. The moon was still there with them, growing slowly pale, as if fatigued by the long night's task of lighting the world. The sea licked the shore with a slow slurp. Nothing violent, nothing dramatic. It was a cove like any other, mild, inoffensive, unpretentiously agreeable.

It's not the way I remember it, thought Felicity. Not at all. Or perhaps it was only the way the beautiful night light was touching it up, lending the shoreline delicacy. The sand was probably still dirty beige, the houses still modest and unimpressive. But in a different way, these days. No clapboard. No flapping doors. No loose shingles. New windows had been fitted and highly unsuitable facing been slapped on the grim facades. Little gardens were surrounded by neat picket fences. Stringy flowers battled with the sea breeze. The residents of Island Park had changed. A new, slightly more affluent, crowd had moved in.

Marek stopped the car, stared out at the landscape of his childhood. What was he feeling? Regret? Horror?

Indifference?

The keys on their chain swung slowly back and forth, back and forth from the ignition.

"It's nicer than the way I remember it," said Felicity to break the silence.

Marek turned, watched her steadily. "It has to be. You hated it so much." And that bothered him, even after all this time.

"And you wanted me to like it?" She looked at him curiously. It had never dawned on her it had been important to him.

"Of course. You saw only ugliness. I wanted to show you magic places."

"Magic places?" She could only remember the drunken father, the martyred mother. Where did magic come into it?

"Of course. Every kid has magic places, an imaginary world. Or perhaps rich little girls growing up in New York don't need that sort of thing?"

"Well, you're wrong," she shot back defiantly. "You still nursing a grudge about my background?"

He reached over and squeezed her hand. "No. I'm not. Go on, tell me about your magic places."

"Okay. I will. Did I ever tell you about my grandfather? The one who used to take me to Central Park?"

"No. Go on."

"I loved him, my grandfather. He told me stories, millions of stories. Adventure stories, stories about people who were stowaways on ships, people who came from places like Siberia. Stories about the far North, the snow, the tundra. He'd been an immigrant from the Russian Pale, and then a pioneer, you see.

He'd been given land to farm by the Canadian government way back when. Before giving it all up and becoming a New York businessman."

"And those stories of far away places must have stimulated your imagination, given you the curiosity to travel."

"I suppose so. Lucky me. But what I remember even more, was what he told me about the rocks."

"What rocks?"

"In Central Park. You see, he told me the rocks were alive. They knew everything that was going on too. They could see, breathe, hear, feel. And they grew. Every day, they grew a little. And I believed him. Each time we came back to the park, I saw they really *were* bigger and bigger." It sounded silly, in the re-telling. She looked at Marek, at his profile. What importance could such a meaningless story have to him? But he turned and smiled, reached for the keys and opened the car door.

"Of course rocks grow. That's how we got the Rockies. Come on. I'll show you my cove."

"Cove?"

"A secret cove. Filled with pirates most of the time." How he'd wanted to show it to her the first time they'd come here, but it had been impossible. He remembered her closed face, her hostility. Strange, being here with her now. As if they were keeping a rain check on a promise made over forty years before.

Scree, pebbles, cracked shells, dried bubbles of blackened seaweed crackled under their feet as they followed the line of the shore toward a low, jagged promontory. The rocks were slippery from the spray, and it was easy to lose their footing. Marek remembered Felicity was only wearing thin ballerina shoes, and he reached down to take her hand, guide her onto the somber mass.

"Just a little further," he encouraged her.

"I'm not worried," she laughed back.

He could see the loose tendrils of hair flying in the wind and had to use his utmost control to stop himself from reaching out, smoothing them back, feeling their softness beneath his fingers.

They had reached the end of the promontory now. The night wind buffeted them, caught them in the rich scent of the sea.

"We can sit here. Look, there's a sort of natural bench carved out."

The bench was narrow, just wide enough to seat the two of them, just narrow enough so they had to sit touching. She could feel the length of his tight thigh against hers, the hardness of a hip. His warmth wafted over her. He smelt wonderful. His neck was so near. What if she leant over and bit it. Or licked it. What would he do?

"Cold?"

"Not at all." Even if she were, she wouldn't have missed this for the world.

"Liar. You're shivering."

"No, I..." She could hardly tell him it was his nearness that was making her tremble.

He slid his arm around her and what was left of her composure shot out into the sky, floated away on the puffing wind. She leaned back against him, blissfully.

"I used to sneak out here a lot," he said, his voice low. "This was where I did my dreaming and planning. When you sit out here, you feel like you're at the edge of the world. That there's nothing else but water out there, no land, no other country, no people. Just water until the earth comes to an end."

"A believer in the flat earth theory, I see." Felicity had to make an effort to keep her teasing tone. She was finding it increasingly hard to keep her thoughts straight.

"Sometimes."

"I'll admit when you're out here nothing seems urgent." She willed herself to relax. If she didn't, then she'd ruin everything. Marek would feel her intensity. Then he'd pull away, remove his arm once again and the magic would be gone, shattered into a billion particles, snatched up by night. "You don't care if the world is round, square, or triangular."

"Until the strange creatures come into view." Marek's tone hinted at unfathomable mysteries. "It looks peaceful enough now, but you'd be surprised at what's out there."

"Peaceful? I wouldn't call a deep, dark, cold ocean peaceful. Tell me about the creatures."

"Crabs. Snails, sea slugs, starfish. Anemones, sea worms, sea cucumbers. There's a whole world palpitating around our feet."

She was aware of his arm tightening around her. Not in a friendly way. But like a lover's.

"Then there are the things that might suddenly appear over the horizon."

"Pirates, you said?" *Hold me tighter, Marek. Really tight*.

"Definitely. In huge ships all flying the Jolly Roger flag. And those pirates are armed to the teeth and as mean as you can get. Naturally, it was up to me to save everyone in the cove from the danger."

"I'll bet the other residents didn't even know they were threatened."

"They certainly didn't. They didn't see a soul."

"Camouflage pirates. Bigger than flies." Nonsense was a pretty good tool when you came down to it, thought Felicity gratefully.

"I even got the occasional visit from Nessie, believe it or not."

"She swam all the way here from Loch Ness just to see you?"

"We had a privileged relationship."

"How about mermaids?"

"No mermaids. Those belong to the dream world of adult males. Lonely sailors on endless voyages." Marek stopped. "Mermaids..."

She could feel his eyes on her, but she didn't dare look up.

"And," he continued softly, "perhaps to middle-aged men who suddenly find themselves dropped into a dream."

"A nice dream?" Felicity's voice was soft and hesitant. She was certain that if he'd been having regrets about bringing her down here again, those regrets were vanishing fast.

What could he answer? He wasn't sure what he wanted anymore. No, that wasn't true either. He knew what he wanted. He knew what he was feeling right now! He had Felicity here, within his grasp. And she was willing, wanting him.

Still, the negative part of his mind insisted on throwing up barriers. What do you and Felicity have in common, it asked him for the thousandth time?

Nothing. Then keep your distance. You pride yourself on being a man who can only be fooled once. Besides, there's no point in getting Felicity's hopes up. Nor his own, for that matter.

So why did he have to fight so hard to keep up this idle chatter? He could hardly think straight watching the way the pale light of impending dawn played across her fine cheekbones. Softened her mouth with subtle shadows. Heaven help him. He was falling under her spell again. Softening. Wanting nothing more than to crush her in his arms, make love to her, right here.

"Listen, Felicity..." He rose abruptly to his feet. *We have to get away from here.* That was what he intended to say. *Let's get back to San Francisco. I'll take you to the airport and we'll go our separate ways.*

Her eyes questioned his as she stood, a slight, graceful woman. And vulnerable, and fragile, hunched against the wind in those thin cotton clothes. He'd only been thinking of himself. She must be freezing and not complaining because she wanted to please him, because she hated to break the mood.

"Come. Let's go back to the car. I can give you my coat, at least." His voice had the note of tenderness he could no longer hide. He held out his hand.

She smiled tremulously, put her hand in his.

Was there anything more satisfying to a man than to know a strong, independent woman was in his power? A woman who wanted him with all her heart and soul. Unable to resist any longer, he put his arms around her, drew her close against his body. With a sigh, she linked her hands around his neck and, with closed eyes, let herself melt into his embrace.

It seemed like hours before she felt his mouth,

before she felt his lips planting one soft kiss on one eyelid, then the other. It was a lifetime before he lowered his mouth to hers.

She couldn't remember any kiss like this. Not in all her memories of the tempestuous and youthful passion she'd shared with him, was there anything like the sheer longing and desire his mouth now expressed. Something wild and tender, demanding and penetrating. His tongue probed with such mastery, she was devoid of will. Knew only that something wonderful was soaring up in her, pinning her to him, making her want more and more.

She sighed softly, fought to get closer to him, struggled to melt against him, arch her hips into his, urge him on, and his answering moan told her he was now beyond resisting her. He was hers. He loved her. She knew it beyond any doubt. She could feel love in the strength of his arms, in his every caress.

"Felicity," he said softly. "My Felicity."

"Marek..."

"Hold it right there! This gun's loaded."

She froze. Felt Marek's body stiffen.

The voice had come from beyond the rocks, somewhere down on the beach. She peered into the distance. The rising sun had thrown its fingers of light onto the indigo sky, and she could just make out the figure of a man. Poised, taut.

With what was—quite definitely—a real gun in his raised arms.

Chapter Nine

Her first tremor of fear gave way to a hopelessness born of serenity. Well, if this was the time to die, it was the right moment. Just when the going was pretty well perfect.

"Now move slowly. Get yerselfs off them there rocks and over heres where I can see you." An old man's voice, she could hear clearly now. Trembling and unsure. Like his fingers on the trigger. Suddenly rage boiled up in her. "You put that gun down this minute."

"Not on yer life, lady. This ain't no Hollywood film."

"Jep?" It was Marek's voice.

There was a long silence. Jep? Who was Jep? Not Marek's father, certainly?

"Jep Wilkins, is that you?"

"Don't you go butterin' me up."

"Jep, it's Marek. Marek Sumner. You remember me, don't you? Danuta and Matt's son."

The next silence was even longer.

"Don't live around here no more."

If the old guy was mad—or senile—they weren't going to survive this.

"Of course they don't." Marek sounded like he was about to laugh. Laugh? Felicity wondered what the joke was.

"Gone."

"Danuta, my mother, has been dead for twenty-seven years. I know that."

There was another long silence. "Either he's still digesting the information, or he's just now worked it out," Felicity muttered.

"Then what you doin' here? You ain't got no business here."

"The beach belongs to everyone, Jep."

"Not this part. This here's mine."

This was grotesque. The only end in sight appeared to be an unpleasant and sticky one. Felicity felt tired, testy. She and Marek had been awake for almost twenty hours. Being at the wrong end of some crank's gun just wasn't her ideal way of starting—or ending—a day.

I've been here before, she thought. She had. And she hadn't liked it one bit—not knowing if you were going to survive an ordeal. She remembered, still, the blazing sun, the dry tickle of wind sending sand scurrying across the floor of the bleached desert. She also remembered exactly how it felt to have a dozen machine guns pointed at your back as you were marched off toward those sinister-looking Moroccan barracks in this wasteland and battlefield of the West Sahara. She'd been part of a convoy bringing medical supplies to Saharouis defending their country from the Moroccans. The Moroccans were making certain no supplies arrived. She heard their gleeful shouts behind her as they unloaded jeeps come so far against all odds.

But this wasn't Morocco. She wasn't part of an international aid program this morning. The situation in Morocco hadn't been fun, but this one wasn't much of a chuckle either. It was one thing risking your skin and knowing exactly what the dangers were; it was quite another finding yourself held hostage simply because you'd been caught spooning on a California beach.

"Now you listen here, Mr. Wilkins, or Jep, or whoever you are," she said angrily. "I've had quite enough. I'm cold. I'm tired. And this situation is ridiculous. I'm going to walk right off this rock and head in the direction of the car. You—" Her tone became commanding. "You are going to put that silly gun down and leave us alone. Go home. Go to sleep. You shouldn't be toddling around at this time of the night—or morning. Not at your age you shouldn't."

There was a strange choking sound, like that of an enraged weasel.

"My age has nothin' to do with it. I'm a fit as you are, you hussy."

She doubted it. The man had a strange way of speaking, as though he were missing a few teeth—or all of them, for that matter. A good set of dentures would work wonders. If she got out of this alive, she'd take the subject up with him.

"Jep?" It was Marek. He really did sound like he was laughing. Perhaps he took violent death as a joke? "Now I know I'm back in Island Park. You haven't held me at the point of a gun for well over fifty years."

"Rotten little thievin' critter you were, too. I should've finished with you back then. Cursed the day yer mother put yer on this here earth."

The situation didn't sound as though it was improving, thought Felicity. She heard a strange rasping sound. A laugh? The old coot was laughing? Or choking with rage.

"Well, you's better come along then. No point standin' out here an' flirtin' with rheumatism. Come on

145

over to the house." The voice took on a sneaky, sly note. "I got some jipple you want to have a taste of."

Whatever jipple might be. Still, things were suddenly—but definitely—looking up. They stepped down on to the scree again, and began to trudge behind the old man, back along the shore in the direction of the houses.

"Lord, Jep. I didn't know you'd still be around," said Marek, a true note of fondness in his voice. Catching up with Jep, he affectionately slung one arm over his stooped shoulder.

"Only the good die young," muttered Jep cantankerously and shook himself free. Nevertheless, the old crank did sound rather chuffed.

Minutes later, they were standing in front of a cottage that looked as though it came out of a strange Slavic fairy tale: the hut of Baba Yaga, the witch, thought Felicity. With certain modifications. There were no chicken claw feet raising it from the ground, but rotten-looking wooden piles.

An evil-sounding door groaned open, and Jep ushered them in.

The only light came from a dirty kerosene lamp that also managed to fill the crazy interior with a nauseous smoke. There were other odors, as well, more complicated ones: rusty metal mixed with strange sea smells, the easily distinguishable tang of distilling alcohol.

So that's what Jep was up to. Brewing illegal alcohol. That's what jipple was, no doubt.

Felicity looked around the room. Pots and pans, bits of wire, cord, strange chunks of metal with no conceivable use or meaning, engine parts, fishnet, gas burners, Bunsen burners, bottles, jugs, lobster pots, crab pots, buckets, hung from nails and hooks planted over every inch of the wooden walls and beams.

"Have a seat, the two of yer. Make yerselves at home." In such a place, the word home took on new meaning.

There were some eight disparate and rickety chairs grouped around a wobbly table. Marek and Felicity sat while Jep shuffled off into some dark corner to deposit his gun and return with three doubtful-looking drinking glasses filled with a strange yellow liquid that smelt anything but tempting.

Felicity could see the old man more clearly now. Scrawny, a two-weeks growth of scruffy beard, he was hook-nosed and beady-eyed. He wasn't entirely toothless—she'd been wrong about that. There was a tooth. One. Long and yellow and sharp.

"Well, nice to see yer again, kid. We'll drink this to old times' sake. Bottoms up."

Bottoms up? Felicity tasted the contents of her glass gingerly and almost fell off her chair as it seared her throat. Jipple tasted like a mixture of diesel fuel, vinegar, sweet apple juice, and very strong rubbing alcohol. It was awful.

Marek sputtered beside her.

"What are you putting in this these days, Jep?"

"None of yer business, young man. It's a secret, and yer knows it is."

And should remain that way. Definitely not for mass production.

"Well, I see you've not lost your touch. It's right up to standard."

"This is a breakfast drink?" Felicity offered

timidly. She was inching her way toward a good excuse for not finishing her glass without offending Jep. She was afraid he'd get annoyed and pull out the gun again. He seemed to be a testy sort of old crock.

"You wimmin folks too wishy-washy for the real stuff, huh?"

"That must be it," she conceded gratefully.

The old man snickered gleefully.

"Only wimmin tough enough was Mae, and she's been gone these many years."

"Your wife?" She was being polite. She tried hard to imagine what sort of woman could ever have lived here. A very peculiar woman, no doubt about it, but jipple would probably make the stoutest soul go odd.

"You young folks don't know nothing," Jep spit out.

She'd offended him, she could see. "Oh. Sorry." Still, it was cute being called young again. At age sixty-three.

"Don't even know who Mae West was, I reckon."

"Mae West? The—um—actress?"

"You betcha. Only was one Mae West."

"You knew Mae West?" Felicity felt like she was taking part in a very strange tea party where normal conversational rules simply didn't apply. Island Park was still hell.

The old man's look was scathing. "Of course I knew Mae West. She was my woman. Years ago now. Why, I remember her sittin' in that very chair where yer sittin' down now."

"Really? How interesting." She wondered how long this particular voyage into total madness was going to last. She felt very tired and wondered if,

148

perhaps, she was even dreaming now. After all, she hadn't totally recovered from traveling halfway across the world. And that sip of the hellish jipple had certainly knocked her for a loop, too.

"It's a well known fact Jep knew Mae West," said Marek. His face was serious enough, but she could see his eyes twinkle. "At least, it's a well known fact here in Island Park."

"Show you a picture, too," said Jep heaving himself to his feet and making his way over to a hunk of battered wooden slats that might—with a great effort of imagination—be called a cupboard. Of sorts. He came back with a curled and yellowing photo, thrust it under Felicity's nose.

The man in the photo might have been Jep—once upon a time. He was handsome then, a thick shock of hair curling over his young man's head. He'd been tall and straight and lean. The blowzy blonde at his side might well have been Mae West. It certainly looked like Mae West—as she'd once been. It could also be someone who looked amazingly like Mae West. They, both of them, stood framed against this very cottage— as it had been some seventy or more years ago. It hadn't changed much: here were the same wooden pile legs, the rotting planks. Amazing, the place was still standing. It was a monument to the stubborn resistance of material against all odds.

"Nice," said Felicity weakly and felt even more wishy-washy.

Jep ignored her. He turned to Marek. "I bet you don't know old Killer Besum died ten years ago. Just keeled over. Doc said it was a case of the bilts."

Didn't surprise her any, Felicity thought. Didn't

threaten her either. You probably had to live in Island Park in order to keel over from the bilts, whatever *that* was. She felt Marek's hand reaching out for hers, and happily she curled her fingers around his. Their kiss back there on the rocks. Now, that had been something! The lazy purl of pure bliss was still winding through her body, and she glanced over at Marek from under her lashes. It was so lovely seeing him there, beside her, the orange light of the lamp playing over his sharp features. No, it was more than lovely. It felt dangerous. And warm. And very exciting.

Marek and Jep had launched into tales of the past. Memories of neighbors long gone. Incidents almost forgotten. At this very moment, life was feeling just fine. She didn't know what was coming, but she wasn't going to let it trouble her now. Eventually, they'd have to sleep. In a bed? A grassy knoll would be fine, a stretch of sand, a forest floor, an artichoke field. With her head cushioned on Marek's shoulder. Her mouth on his.

"Yer folks thinking of stayin' around a few days?" Jep's question cut into thoughts bordering on steamy.

"Here? In Island Park?"

"What's wrong with Island Park?"

"Nothing, Jep," Marek began. "It's just that—"

Jep cut him off abruptly. "Yer beach house is still standin'."

"My beach house?" The astonishment was clear in Marek's voice. "You've got to be kidding!"

"No kiddin'. I takes care of the place for ye. Reckoned yer'd be back one day."

"I don't rightly know what to say."

Felicity watched surprise war with tenderness on

Marek's face. "What beach house?"

"Nothin' to say." Jep was getting emotional, too. "Can stay out there if you want."

"After all this time."

"Years, you ain't come back here, boy." There was a note of hurt accusation in his voice. Heaving himself out of his chair, Jep shuffled over to a nail on the wall, took down a huge key, gnarled and complicated. "Place gonna be musty."

Musty? After years, the word musty was going to be inappropriate.

"What beach house?" Felicity asked again.

"Come. I'll show you."

Full daylight had arrived, snuck in quietly while they'd sat in Jep's cabin. A typical seaside morning, salty, cool, breezy, the air hazy, the sky the palest blue above a somber sea. Marek led Felicity past a curious pair of sagging, weather-beaten, old-fashioned outhouses with half-moons carved into their doors, then along a barely discernible dirt lane zigzagging in a southerly direction and following the line of the ocean.

"Did Jep really know Mae West?"

Marek shrugged. "Who knows? Who cares? Jep thinks he did, and he's the only person it matters to."

"True. Truth being relative, even in the best of situations." Her feet in the ballerina shoes were finding the path hard going.

Thirsty-looking weeds sprouted between damp-looking rocks. Just ahead, a lone wooden structure loomed. It resembled a fisherman's hut made out of all manner of planks grown dark from the constant assault of salty waves. A beautiful and utterly spontaneous arrangement of wild flowers and sea grasses nestled against it, as if seeking shelter from the constant wind. There was a tiny verandah, two shuttered windows and a sturdy wooden door. Marek slid the key into the lock.

The interior was simplicity itself. A scrubbed wooden table, chairs, a bed with a rolled back mattress. There, along one wall, were wooden cupboards.

"I made those things," he said, his voice strangely tight. "So long ago. From all the odds and ends of planks I found washed up along the shoreline."

"You spent a lot of time here?" It must have meant a lot to him, this cabin. Felicity could read it on his face.

"It was a crazy idea of mine, fixing up this abandoned old hut. As a kid, I needed a place I could go to and be safe from my father's drunken rages. And Jep sensed that. He's an old crank, but he took care of me. Taught me things about the sea, the tides. Taught me how to build things, use my hands." His voice was filled with tenderness.

For a place so long ago abandoned, there was relatively little dust. The old man had obviously been keeping it up. It probably meant a lot to him, as well.

"This is wonderful," breathed Felicity, and she saw the pleasure in his eyes.

"You really like it?"

"Why would I lie?"

"To please me." His grin turned wicked.

"Stop being so sure of yourself!" She looked at him accusingly. "Why didn't you show me this the last time we were here?"

"What would you have said if I had?"

She reflected for a minute. "Don't know. Probably I would have liked it then, too."

"Do you like it enough to spend tonight here with me?"

"Here?" Her voice had the edge of a squeak to it. "Here? You mean...Together? Now? Tonight?" Her heart began the usual slow pound when she connected thoughts of close proximity with Marek.

"We could leave."

"Oh no, we can't," she said quickly. Too quickly. She was sounding positively lecherous, she realized. She tried to regain her dignity by throwing him a cool, detached look.

He'd started laughing.

"Wait a minute, Marek. We don't have sheets, or blankets. Essentials..."

"No problem. I have a sleeping bag in the car."

She stared. "A sleeping bag?" He'd been planning this out? Really? Since when?

"Right. A sleeping bag."

"*One* sleeping bag?"

"Right again." A slow smile crossed his face.

"Marek Sumner. Do you know what kind of risk you're running?"

"I do. You've been warning me ever since we met up again."

"Good." She laughed, shakily. "I wasn't sure the message was really getting across."

"Then I'll go get our things from the car. Sit down. I'll be right back."

Sit down. As if she could.

She was suddenly nervous. Very nervous. How could she just go and sit down? She checked out other possible modes of behavior. She could strip off her clothes and wait for Marek's reappearance. That way there'd be no mistaking exactly what was going to happen with two of them in one sleeping bag. But that sounded a little too drastic as far as tactics went.

Make yourself useful instead.

She threw open the wooden shutters and the delicate, cerulean morning sky slipped into the room, touched up the dark wood with its soft, hazy fingers. She rolled back the mattress, sniffed. It had a faint sea smell, but it wasn't musty. Just damp. Nothing a stretch in the sun wouldn't cure.

She told her hands to stop shaking. My goodness. She was sixty-three years old now, and Marek was an old friend—almost. Why did she feel as though she was around seventeen and just about as inexperienced. This was a fling for old time's sake, wasn't it? A bit of unfinished business from the past. In a few days time, it would be all over, and she and Marek would get back to their own separate lives. *And don't you dare get depressed about that, Felicity Powers. Life goes on in a forward direction, not backward. And time is very definitely not consecutive!*

****

He saw her as he came over the little rise of sand. She was out there, crouched down low in the sea, the gleam of her hair like a foaming whitecap against the darkness of a wave. Just as he'd hoped all those years ago, a real mermaid had finally appeared. Or perhaps a sea goddess. The inconsequence of his thoughts almost made him laugh with joy.

It must be freezing, the water. The Pacific was never warm up here.

He stopped, gazed out at her, looked away, looked back again. He was doomed. He knew it. His heart beat wildly, painfully, and his soul turned over. Slowly, he forced himself to enter the cottage, drop the bags on the floor. Pulling off his clothes seemed to take an incredible effort. Always the same awkward things, buttons, zippers, and sleeves.

She was watching him, her eyes luminous, dark, when he waded into the ocean, and as he approached her, she stood. Her body was angular and palely glistening. The same body he'd known and loved. Familiar. Soft, and trembling, and utterly beautiful.

This was really happening. This really was Marek coming toward her. Marek who was about to take her into his arms. This wasn't a dream, she told herself and still, she could hardly allow herself to believe. She was terrified if she took her eyes away, he'd vanish. That he was merely a mirage, that in an instant he'd turn into a ghostly cloud of sea spray.

But he wasn't a mirage, and he came closer and closer now. He really was here. She took in his narrow hips, long, lean, muscled legs, his maleness showing her how much he wanted her, that his desire matched hers.

"Oh, Marek," she breathed. "You're so beautiful." Her face was upturned, her eyes half-closed and filled with desire for him.

He laughed. "I'm beautiful? I should be the one who's saying that."

"But you are. You are," she moaned, her voice husky with want. Her fingers reached out, traced the long line of his shoulder.

His eyes watched her face, fascinated. "Beautiful Felicity. The way I've always remembered you."

"Have you remembered me often?" Her eyes

glinted suddenly. Wickedly, provocatively.

"More often than you'll believe."

"You did?" It was all she wanted to hear. All she'd hoped for.

Then he whispered her name and lifted her head and held it cupped in his hands as he looked at her. "I've dreamed about you more nights than you'll ever know. You were trouble from the first second I set eyes on you all those years ago."

She saw how true the words were in the green glitter of his eyes, saw the passion burning deep inside him. "I never want to forget this moment," she said softly. She studied his face, the strong cheekbones, the rugged, square jaw softened now by faint beard stubble. She reached up and traced the line of his wonderful mouth with the tip of one salty finger. "Such a beautiful mouth," she murmured. "So beautiful."

She slid her fingers across the tight skin of his shoulders, slowly caressed the back of his neck, knotted themselves in the rich curl of his hair. He bent down and kissed her then with all the passion his heart and soul could hold.

Felicity nearly swooned as desire burst through her. Her body arched, her hips pressed against his in a demand and need that was unmistakable. She needed to feel him inside of her, filling her. She wanted him deep in her body. Snaking one leg around his hip so her intimacy touched his, she, invited, coaxed, guided.

"No," he whispered, gazing down at her through a haze of passion. "Not here. Not yet. This is going to go slowly, Felicity. Very, very slowly. I'm going to taste you, every single part of you." He reached up into the glow of her hair and loosened the clips holding it in place. Just like he'd done all those years ago. A gesture his fingers had never forgotten.

Her hair tumbled down over her shoulders, a rippling gleaming mane. She looked up, laughed and his eyes dropped to her breasts, full with passion, their nipples erect, waiting for his mouth to cover them. Effortlessly, he gathered her into his arms, and began to carry her back through the waves that swirled around his legs, back in the direction of the cottage.

"I'm glad you're doing this," she murmured against his shoulder. "My knees have gone all odd." Nestled against his shoulder, she could take the soft skin of his neck between her teeth.

"Keep on doing that, and we'll never make it to the cottage. My knees feel as odd as yours."

"I don't care if we do. Just as long as I can have you anyway. And anywhere." The thought made her giddy. "All of you."

"Shameless woman."

The bed was waiting for them, and he laid her down softly, watched her, wanting to see her, wanting to be certain this was reality.

"Come," she whispered, reaching out for him. "I want to taste you. I want to explore every inch of you again with my tongue." But she didn't know if she could wait that long. Not this time. Not now. She wanted him too much, and he knew it.

He buried his face in her hair. It smelt wonderful, rich, deep, secret. He savored the sea-washed delicacy of her skin, drew his mouth down over the softness of her belly to the silky junction between her thighs. "Skin like hot silk," he sighed. He felt her melt against him, felt the shiver racing through her flesh, heard her call out his name, cling to him, lost in the frenzy only he knew how to create in her.

She would return all the pleasure he was giving her. She would love, tease, and caress until his control over his emotions shattered. Together they would tumble into ecstasy, stronger and more powerful than it had ever been. She would drag him with her to the boundaries of desire, pull him into the world of joy and fulfillment so he would never be able to forget her. Never stop thinking about her in his dreams. Never cease to want her.

And this was only the beginning.

****

Felicity woke to the heavenly scent of Marek's skin. Her head was resting on his shoulder, her cheek rubbing the hardness of his chest.

In the haze of the late afternoon sun, she remembered, dreamlike, what had happened over the last few hours. Marek. Beside her.

They'd woken at noon, and in the raw blaze of the mid-daylight, made love again, deeply, intensely, as if trying to store enough memories to carry them through the next forty years. Or a lifetime.

Because this would end.

The thought jerked Felicity back into the here and now, back into full consciousness. Endings? She didn't want to think about endings when this seemed like a beginning. She didn't want to think at all.

"Marek?"

He was awake. Smiling down at her, with eyes so tender, so soft, so loving. No. This had nothing to do with endings.

"Hi." He ran a lazy hand over her breasts, and she

curled toward him, her body still registering desire.

"Have you been awake long?" She felt the shy confusion of a woman new to a man's intimacy: strange, wonderful, foolish.

"Some time." He smiled, nuzzling her. "I liked watching you sleep. Dream."

She felt embarrassed. "Hope I didn't snore."

"Like the leading lady in an enchanted dream." He drew her close.

That's what she felt like, too.

"Do you know what time it is?"

She blinked. Judged the light. "Three in the afternoon? Four?"

"Seven."

"Seven o'clock? In the evening?"

"We burned up the best part of the day in a rather special way. Remember?" His eyes teased.

"I remember, all right." Her hand slid over his chest, delicately, her fingers tracing the line of a nipple. Pleasure warmed his face, and he laughed quietly. She loved his grin, she loved the way his eyes crinkled at the corners. Fine lines, age lines denoted time past, a past that had nothing to do with her. *A whole life that had nothing to do with me.*

Could you fall in love with the same person twice? For her, things were easy. She'd never been out of love with Marek. What about him? What was he feeling?

"What's going to happen to us?"

The bright green of his eyes darkened. "Us? Do we have to plan?"

There it was. The essential difference between men and women. Women give themselves totally, without compromise. Men hold themselves back. Avoid commitment.

"I suppose not. But it would be nice if we could do this kind of thing more often."

"It would be." He sounded speculative, as if he were mulling the idea over in his head for the first time.

"It still works, doesn't it? There's still magic between us."

"Magic? Very definitely magic. Other things, too." He kissed her shoulder marveling at the softness of her skin. "And it's not over yet."

Her heart fluttered. "Thank goodness for that."

"How about if we stay here for the next few days?" His voice was deep, husky enough to send shivers down her spine. "Would you be willing to do that with me?"

"You think I could refuse?"

"I'm vain enough to think you won't be able to." He kissed her forehead, her nose, the softness of her neck under the warm curtain of hair. "Even though there's no electricity, no running water, and no luxury."

"You're right. I won't refuse." She slid her leg slowly over his hips. "I'm even willing to make another rendezvous."

"What rendezvous?" His eyes glinted.

"We can do this again in forty years time. Although, I have to warn you. By then I'll be even older than Grandma Moses. And I'll probably look it, too."

"Great-grandma Moses meets Great-grandpa Moses for a torrid weekend." He chuckled. "I'm looking forward to it."

Chapter Ten

For three days and nights, life mainly consisted of lovemaking interspersed with meals at the nearby Dewdrop Inn—food neither Felicity nor Marek felt hungry enough to appreciate. Their one real hunger was for each other; sometimes they barely made it back to the privacy of the cabin, so urgent was their need for contact, so intense was the burning that raged through them. But there were also forays for buckets of fresh water from the open tap behind Jep's hut, and occasional but exceptionally strange chats with Jep himself. Felicity was even getting used to the wicked jipple Jep always insisted on pouring out for her. She couldn't say she liked it—that would be going too far. In all honesty, she could only say she hated it less.

But tonight, Marek announced she'd better dress up; they were going out for a fancy candlelit dinner in Monterey—just as a contrast to life in a hut with nothing but stone age comfort.

"But I don't own any dressy things," Felicity informed him. And, only after much digging around in that chaotic big blue bag of hers, did she finally pull out just another simple white Indian cotton shirt, another full skirt, and another pair of flat ballerina shoes. It was the best she could do, she explained apologetically.

And dressed like that, she looked wonderful too, Marek thought. She didn't need designer clothes: just the way she carried herself would make a frock in plastic webbing look fashionable. And why was he really insisting on this night out?

"I want to offer you a bit more of the luxury I couldn't afford back then," he found himself explaining as they wandered through town, surveying chic restaurants and expensive boutiques. But he hardly recognized the place now. "Forty-something years ago, I'd have given anything to have been able to invite you to a restaurant in Monterey for dinner. And I felt like a failure because I couldn't."

Felicity looked at up at him with sympathy. "I don't think you ever told me, you know. If you had, I'd have pointed out that things like dinners in classy restaurants didn't matter to me. Not back then, and not now either."

"I know. *Now*, I know. But I couldn't really understand such things back then. Material goods never mattered to you because you'd always had them. But I'd grown up in a house where bills were never paid, where meals largely consisted of Brussels sprouts stolen from the fields, and knowing my mother and I risked waking up on the street because my father had caroused away the welfare money again. Therefore, my idea of success meant having enough cash in my wallet to wine and dine you." He grinned. "At least once."

"Well, I suppose tonight's the night." She smiled back at him. "Call it cashing in a rain check."

He looked at her, his heart full, knowing his defenses were down. Only temporarily, of course. But it was a dangerous game, all the same. Yet why fight temptation? Why fight Felicity? These days together were a lovely, lazy interval in his life. One he was happy he hadn't denied himself, one he'd always remember. Yet soon enough it would be over. He'd be returning to the real world, his real life, his home in Connecticut, his work, and his self-imposed isolation.

He chose a restaurant close to Cannery Row for their dinner. There were crisp white tablecloths, lit candles, and cut flowers in the little vases on each table. The white wine they were drinking was fragrant and delicious; their table overlooked the sea; the food on the menu was tempting. Yes, all the elements of luxury were there, all right. But, strangely enough, this experience didn't seem to be half as romantic as the last few evenings he'd spent with Felicity in that one-room beach shack in Island Park.

He watched her now, saw her looking around the room. "This restaurant was here in the old days, wasn't it? I seem to remember it."

"It was," he answered soberly. "I'm wondering if it wasn't a simpler place back then, though. But who knows? When you look at things from the outside, pressing your nose against the glass, wanting what you can't have, everything looks more wonderful."

"Wonderful?" She shrugged. "I wonder. Oh, I'm pretty certain our meal will be delicious—everything smells so good. But you know what? As nice as this restaurant is, I love spending the evenings in your rattling old hut, just the two of us, drinking wine by the light of that very stinky kerosene lamp. It's even more luxurious than this, somehow."

"I'm glad you think so," he said, deeply touched, his voice strangely soft. "I was thinking exactly the same thing. Less than a minute ago."

She stared at him her brown eyes flickering. Then

shook her head wonderingly. " It's odd, isn't it: we've been separated for all these years; the lives we've lived have been so disparate; yet we're still so familiar to each other, and so similar."

It was true; she was absolutely right. But their differences were still as strong as ever, too. He wanted her to realize that. Just so she wouldn't be disappointed when they separated again. Because, knowing Felicity, she probably thought fairy tales could go on forever.

He knew better. Of course he did. He knew long-term relationships very rarely worked—look at the disaster his parents' marriage had been. And his own marriage to Nathalie had ended in divorce. And Felicity's. Okay, both he and Felicity had certainly married the wrong people for the wrong reasons, but what had happened to his own relationship with Felicity? All those years ago, they'd been together for all the right reasons—love, passion, intellectual stimulation—yet they'd also separated. And would again, if they tried to live together. He was certain of it.

But why think about separation now? Why feel sad? He was here; she was here. They loved each other, that was clear enough. Not that he could come out and say it. If he did, she'd certainly think he meant permanence.

He looked over at her now, smiled. "I'm even willing to bet you wouldn't mind spending the rest of your life in a hut without electricity. And you'd never even complain. Am I right?"

"Probably." She nodded. "But, then again, I'm used to that sort of thing. In most of the places I've lived in, there's only intermittent electricity and very rarely good water."

"And so you always adjust. Stay flexible."

"Like any decent aid worker would," she said soberly. "I'm not any different from the others. Because we're always moving around, we have to be able to adjust to new cultures very quickly. And by remaining flexible, we can live in frankly awful conditions and not let it bother us. Besides, the last thing anybody needs in dangerous situations is a complainer. Or someone who's untrustworthy. Because the job requires handling large amounts of money and supplies."

"Tell me more about what you were doing."

Her hands came up in a gesture of frustration. "I wouldn't even know where to begin. I know most people think humanitarian aid consists in nothing more than handing over food and water to smiling grateful people, then sitting under coconut trees gurgling at babies and gossiping with local women. Of course there's a tiny bit of that some of the time, but mostly, an aid worker has to fight tragedy, conflict, poverty, disaster, horror, and famine. And one way of doing it is by writing proposals and reports, by analyzing budgets, monitoring data, and dealing with headquarters. On top of that, you're confronted by incredible corruption and greed. And then there's grueling travel and horrific danger."

"And because you're Felicity, because you're tough and adventurous, you can do it." He admired her; he'd always admired her. But didn't she see she came from another constellation, one very foreign to him? One light years away and perfectly inaccessible to him.

But she only shrugged, as if the characteristics he credited her with were of no real importance. "Of course, sometimes there are other jobs we have to do, too. Less dangerous ones. Once, I ran a local radio station in Burundi. During the war there."

He shook his head regretfully. "Sure you did. During a *war*." Why didn't she understand?

****

The night was still warm by the time they left the restaurant. Marek fetched a flashlight from the car. "Now I can finally show you the best part of Monterey. The tide pool life. It's even more spectacular here than it is in Island Park. Actually, it's the real reason I brought you down here."

"You didn't bring me here for dinner?"

"Dinner was just to kill time until low tide. The really good stuff is waiting just over those rocks…if you think you can manage clambering over them in those pretty little shoes."

She sniffed. "Stop underestimating my talent for fancy footwork."

"I'd never be silly enough to do that," he answered wryly. But he kept his arm wound tightly around her. Just in case she slipped. Or just in case she eluded his grasp for even one moment. That, he didn't want to happen.

They went down to where gentle waves licked at the rocky shoreline. Stopped when they were far out enough to reach a pool of water just recently revealed by the sea.

"Now we're going to spy on the invertebrates, animals without backbones. People usually don't pay much attention to them. Take this character, for example." He pointed.

"A snail," said Felicity. She didn't sound in the least impressed.

166

"Sure. You can be bored by a snail if you want, because seeing them is an everyday, banal experience. But once you know a few things, you'll never look at a snail in the same way again."

"I'm game. Go on."

"Well, they have eyes on their tentacles, a mouth, and a sharp saw-like instrument called a radula they use for scraping, grasping, biting, tearing flesh, rasping, and boring through shells. Most snails close up their shells with a trap-door called an operculum, but their cousins, the limpets, only have flat cap shells. Just so they won't dry out at low tide, limpets have to go home to a specific site they've carved out in a rock." He laughed briefly. "That description could also be applied to me and to my own lifestyle."

"That's better than having a trap door?"

"Am I boring you?"

Felicity curled her fingers through his. "No. You aren't. But I do feel ignorant, suddenly."

He was pleased he could tell her things she didn't know. Could find territory on which she was less sure—just the way he felt when she talked about exotic parts of the world. He trained the flashlight on a small, reddish mass. "Look, Felicity. This is a sponge. It has no internal organs, no muscles and no nerves. It spends its life attached to a rock. Most are hermaphrodites, produce both eggs and sperm. They broadcast sperm into the water, and it's taken in by other female-stage sponges to fertilize their eggs."

"Not much effort involved. Probably not much pleasure either."

"Who knows? Pleasure is always relative anyway." He stood, led her to another pool, one further out. "This is an anemone colony, and all these anemones are genetically identical. Each colony defends its territory against other anemone clones."

"Sounds very much like human society," she mused.

"I suppose that's the whole point of this exercise," Marek responded dryly. "Tide pools are a microcosm: a world reflecting our own."

She looked up at him. "And if you're a limpet, what am I?"

"You? You're a beautiful sea star, living way out there, where the water's deep and the waves are violent."

"Stop putting distance between us." She shook her head, laughed briefly. "Where did you learn about marine animals anyway?"

"At home. In Island Park. When I was a little kid. Jep taught me some things. The school library and the science teacher taught me more. And I learned the rest just by observing these creatures."

"But you never shared the information with me."

"No. I didn't. I guess I didn't think you'd be interested. Or perhaps it was my secret world and I didn't want to share it. You see, when I became too old to believe in pirate ships, marine life not only became my reality, it was also my alternative world. I could walk out of my front door, leave the all the shouting and insults behind me, and retreat to the relative silence of tide pool life, only a dozen yards away."

He stopped, closed his eyes. Took in a deep breath of the salty sea air. Felt the compelling warmth of Felicity's body beside him, the pleasure of her fingers curled together with his. "Except, I know one thing now: I was right to believe in mermaids and sea goddesses."

She rested her head on his shoulder. Sighed. "Of course you were, Poseidon."

"Poseidon? Not a very nice god."

"A breaker of hearts," she agreed. "But also Medusa's passionate lover. Did you ever think of studying marine biology instead of literature?"

"I did," he admitted. "But for me, the lure of the world of imagination was just that bit stronger than pure science."

"Because you're a romantic."

"Is that how you see me?" he asked. He was suddenly uncomfortable. A romantic? Perhaps he had been. Once. But not any more. Those days were over with. "I'm too old to be a romantic now."

"Because romance has an age issue?"

And that would lead to a discussion he preferred to avoid at the moment. He stood, pulled her to her feet. "Come on. We still have one more rain check to catch up on."

"We do? Which one?"

"One I was stupid enough to pass up on a few days ago."

"Meaning?"

He didn't answer: it wasn't really a situation for words.

****

He'd seen the untended garden earlier, as they'd walked through town. It had been early evening then, and the roses, the wild vegetation, had been caught in the last rays of the sun. Did it belong to anyone, or was it just another forgotten paradise, one that would soon disappear, ground up by a bulldozer's teeth? Could he even find the place again now that night had fallen? He had to!

Yes, here it was. He stopped in the deep shadow of a tangled hedge: once a narrow wooden gate had barred entry, but it had long since sagged into uselessness.

"What is this place?" Felicity asked

"Worried?"

"Hardly," she scoffed.

"A forgotten garden."

The moon touched all with its delicate silvery light, and the perfume of heavy, half-wild flowers filled the salty night air. They pushed through the vegetation, reached the center of this garden from the past. Wind-blown roses nodded beside an overturned birdbath; a carved stone bench lay half-hidden by fragrant honeysuckle.

"What a wonderful place," Felicity breathed. "I wish I knew its story. Who it belonged to. Why it was abandoned."

He shrugged. "We'll probably never know. You do know why I've brought you here, though."

"No. Tell me."

"To hold you in my arms in a garden filled with roses. To love you with only the stars as witness, just the way I did all those years ago."

Her eyes glittered and she turned into him. "A bed isn't good enough for you?" she asked huskily.

"Oh, it is. Making love with you is wonderful anywhere. But this is a rain check. From the other night. In San Francisco." His voice was as husky as hers. "When we were in the taxi, and we passed the garden where we'd spent the night together years ago."

She rubbed her cheek against his chest, and her warm sigh was one of desire and submission. "And the other night, you could have stopped that taxi. I'd have clambered over that fence with you then and there, you know."

"Yes, I know. Now I know. But you said nothing then."

"How could I? One minute you were there with me; seconds later, you were so distant."

"And I've hated myself ever since for letting the opportunity pass."

She laughed softly. "And you were the one who said you weren't a romantic?"

For a minute he was still, wanting only to see her standing there, etched by the moon's iridescent beams. Then, in that gesture so familiar to him, so gentle, he reached up, loosened the barrettes holding her hair, watched the curls tumble down over her shoulders. Filling his hands with its chaotic wildness, he bent, rested his forehead against hers.

Unbelievable. This whole situation was unbelievable. He was here with Felicity. Again. After all this time. And nothing had changed, nothing had been lost: not their desire, not their love, not their need, not their compassion for one another.

"Sometimes miracles do happen," he half whispered. A deep, rolling wave of tenderness filled his heart, and he pulled her closer, folding her tightly against him, feeling the beating of her heart against his.

"As if our coming together again is the most natural thing in the world," she murmured gently. "Even our souls seem to be intimately and eternally bound."

The words floated on the air. She was right, he thought. Their souls had been bound together from the very first instant they'd met.

And then reality intruded. Their souls? Nonsense. It was this situation that provoked thoughts like that. The clear night, the fragrant forgotten garden, the timeless sound of distant waves, the waxy veil of moonlight.

But he continued to hold her, loving her warmth, her being. And if his idea had been to make love under a starry sky, this moment had little to do with desire, and everything to do with tenderness.

Chapter Eleven

"Tell me about your marriage," Felicity asked. She was utterly naked and lying in the sand in front of the beach house, in the shade of the long grasses shuddering in the buffeting sea breeze.

"What do you want to know?"

"Basic things. How long were you married? Who was she?" Her tone was light and her manner relaxed, but the wary look in her eyes betrayed her.

"It seems like all that happened in another life," he answered slowly. "One belonging to someone else." He was naked, too. And so beautiful. Sitting there, right above her, in that chair tipped back against the railing of the tiny verandah. The hair on his chest followed an enticing line down to his belly, curled deliciously around his manhood. His legs, long, endless, were stretched out in front of him to catch the sun.

Felicity lifted her head slightly so she could study, one more time, his face. Sharp, strong cheekbones, the flash of his eyes under the half-closed lids, the sensuous mouth that brought her so much pleasure she trembled just thinking about it. "Marek?" She couldn't stop herself from saying it. "I don't think I'll ever get tired of gawking at you. You are such a gorgeous hunk of man." As soon as she'd said the words, she regretted them. They had the ring of permanence about them. They held wishes.

If he'd noticed, he didn't let on. Instead, he grinned. "Just keep on thinking that." What was that? A promise? Or just small talk?

The beach was, as usual, completely deserted. No one came over in this direction. Felicity thought about Jep, his gun, and his illegal whiskey. If anyone could keep away nosy trespassers, Jep could—and that was a real blessing. She and Marek could lie here, their bodies bared to the warm, salty air, hearing nothing but the waves and the wind. She'd always known this was what luxury was really about. Not those consumer trappings of clothes, fast, expensive cars, fine restaurants, designer interiors, clubs and chic resorts.

"Come on, Marek. Stop hedging. Tell me about your wife."

"My wife? Rather my ex-wife." Marek shrugged. "You really want to know?"

"I really want to know."

He looked vaguely out to sea. "We were good in bed."

Felicity stiffened. Did she really want to know this after all? She wasn't so sure anymore.

"Very good, actually," he continued, slowly. "Even at the end of the relationship when we had nothing else to say to each other. That's probably why we married in the first place. Passion." He stopped and his mouth twisted wryly. "Of course she did also like the idea of being married to a burgeoning and potentially very successful author. That sort of thing always has been an erotic stimulant for Nathalie."

"Oh," Felicity said faintly. Then added in a voice as neutral as possible in order not to sound catty. "She was a groupie?"

"My agent."

"Oh." She swallowed. "Uh, what did she look like?" Although she'd seen a picture of the woman in a newspaper article long ago.

"She looked good."

Damn! "Go on. I want the gory details." If she were going to suffer, she'd do it in a big way.

"Is this just raw curiosity, Felicity?"

"No way. It's pure masochism."

He chuckled softly. "Don't worry. Nathalie was a totally different type from you. No. I've got that the wrong way around. You're the totally different one." His eyes played over her long, sun and shade-dappled body. "Nathalie is very ambitious. And small, dark haired, compact. You, on the other hand..."

"I'm still a string bean. But an older one."

"Stop fishing. You know what I think about you, about your body."

She did. She'd heard the words he'd used when they made love. He'd also told her he'd never been with a woman who had responded to his own desire with such intensity. That it had never been so good for him. Ever. But those were words said in the heat of passion. Wonderful words. Only he'd left out the way he felt about her, Felicity, pleasures of the body put aside. About that, he was silent. *And you're not going to think about that either. You are not going to ruin this idyll.*

"What went wrong in your marriage?"

"Nothing. Aside from the fact we discovered we had nothing to say to each other than details about negotiating contracts. The marriage was a mistake from the beginning. One lasting eleven years."

"A fairly long mistake." She turned on her side and

175

watched him intently.

"We kept up the façade of a marriage because of Daniel, our son."

"I see."

"Don't forget, I knew how devastating the effect of not having a father—or rather, having the worst kind of father—could be on a boy. So I was determined to stick it out with Nathalie for years. Long after the rightful end of the relationship."

"Eleven years? Surely your son wasn't old enough by then to accept you were separating?"

"No. But when things became intolerable, Nathalie and I decided the best solution was to divorce but still stay in the same neighborhood. That way Daniel felt he had both parents on hand."

"And then?"

"And then what?"

Felicity sat up, glared at him with frustration. "Come on, Marek. Getting you to talk about yourself is like pulling teeth. What sort of life did you have after splitting up with Nathalie? What's your life like now? What's your environment like? What women have you known? How many times have you fallen in love? You know what I mean. Stop this hedging."

Marek grinned wryly. "How much time do I have? You're asking me to detail the last thirty years."

"I certainly am. So start now."

"Or you're not letting me off this beach."

She didn't answer, but folding her arms across her chest, looked at him ferociously. And waited.

He watched her, his mouth still smiling, his eyes warm and filled with something that looked a lot like love. "Do you know how beautiful you are?" he asked softly. "No hair dye, no makeup, no reticence. You have the courage to be natural, to be you, to do what you want. The strength to live with insecurity. But me? I'm an old stick-in the-mud. I always have been. I'm the sort of person who only dreams of doing what you've done in your lifetime. I sometimes think about the things I wish I had the courage to attempt. And then I just stay home, do research, prepare to write another book."

"But your books have depth. You need courage to write about the things you do," she protested. "You take risks, too. Some critics have been ferocious about your work."

"Courage?" He looked doubtful. Then shook his head. "Perhaps. But I don't really see it that way; I feel as though I've been confronting my own immobility all my life. When you left for Paris all those years ago, one part of me wished I could give everything up, go and join you. Live a hand-to-mouth existence, too. Take risks. And the other part of me, the serious stick-in-the-mud part, kept me right here. Got me into a marriage without love in it, brought out a need to be a good father and to stick with the goal."

"And then?"

"And then what?"

"There have been scads of other women since your divorce, I suppose."

"Of course there have been other women in my life. Why shouldn't there have been? I'm not the pope. And, yes, I've known some very nice women. Intelligent, warm women. I enjoyed being with them, doing things with them." He stopped.

A faint line of cloud doodled itself across the

horizon. Felicity took a deep breath. "Doing things with them? Enjoyed being with them? That's all? You never thought of falling madly in love and marrying again? Or just living with someone. Or making a commitment?"

"I never met anyone else I wanted to live with for the rest of my life." He said it calmly, quietly.

That was meant for her, too. Obviously. Despite the great sex. Sex probably even better than it had been with Nathalie. "There must be a vast ragged heap of broken hearts lying around somewhere," she said, keeping her voice as cool as his, but hating herself for the banality of those hackneyed words. Of course, none of this was any of her business. And if she'd been smart enough to keep her mouth shut, not ask all those questions, she wouldn't be hurting like this either.

"I never promised something I knew I wouldn't be able to give."

Well, if anything made things clear, that did. It reduced their coupling to just that. Sex. Wildly exciting, terrifyingly powerful…but, ultimately speaking, empty. As far as he was concerned, that was. As far as her own feelings went? Well, frankly, her own heart had just dropped onto that big banal and sloppy pile of broken ones. The worst of it was, she had no one to blame but herself. As usual. She was the one who'd been determined to seduce him. She was the one who'd come galloping over the horizon, all set to re-conquer.

"Phooey."

"Phooey, what?" His green eyes glinted curiously.

"Nothing. Just an internal debate." She hadn't even known she'd spoken out loud. *What you are not going to do, is come out with wild declarations of love*, she commanded herself. *That, I forbid you to do, Felicity Powers*.

"Marek?"

"Yes?"

Damn! If only the sound of his voice wasn't so musical. If only she didn't love hearing his words. If only she didn't respect him. If only he bored her silly. If only he wasn't so much a part of her. If only...

"Marek, for what it's worth..." She kept her eyes squeezed shut. She couldn't look at him. She couldn't.

"Yes?"

"Marek. I do love you. Very, very much."

There was a long silence. A very painful one. She couldn't stand this one minute longer. She jumped to her feet inelegantly.

"Well," she said briskly. "Now that's over with, so we can think about what we're having for dinner. Will we go back to the Dew Drop Inn again, or shall we—"

"Felicity!" He stood, grabbed her before she could race into the relative safety of the cabin. She struggled to get away, but he folded his arms around her, held her close. "Felicity," he breathed into her hair. "I know you love me. I'm glad you do."

"Oh, how *nice* of you to be glad," she said bitterly.

"And you know I love you, too."

Her heart stopped. "I do? I mean, you do?"

"Of course I do."

What did that mean? Was she back in the role of the beloved family dog again? But it wasn't a question she could ask. Either the person you loved offered the information of their own free will, or you groped about in the dark, bumping into doubts, straddling misery, cracking your head against fear.

"Oh," she murmured.

"I always have loved you."

"Oh," she said again. The brilliance of her repartee was plunging her into the depths of despair. Try though she might, she couldn't do better. Her brain had ceased to produce coherent thought. Temporarily, at least. She buried her face in his shoulder. He smelt so wonderful. Musky, slightly sweaty. Powerful.

"That's the tragic side of our relationship."

"Tragic?" She was really starting to hate herself.

"We love each other. We want each other. We only have to do this—" He stopped, ran a lazy finger along her collarbone, down between her breasts. "Just that, and desire starts again."

He was right. It did. Her legs began wobbling; her hips arched into him.

"It's just that we can't live together. We're too different. It would be impossible. Disastrous. You can see that, can't you?"

The erotic reactions vanished. "Nope."

Marek sighed. The same sigh he'd give when coping with a wayward child. Still, she wasn't going to make this easy for him. Why should she?

"Okay. Let's talk." He sat down again, pulled her onto his lap with the usual strength and ease he always displayed. "You want to know about my life, right? Well, it's anything but exciting. Or perhaps I should say, to me it's exciting enough. But it wouldn't be for anyone else. Especially you. I know you well enough to know my sort of life would drive you crazy. I live way out in the country, in an old rattling farmhouse. There are no neighbors, and there's no real social life. I have all my greatest conversations with birds, the deer, snakes, mosquitoes, and raccoons."

"Doesn't sound bad to me," she said in a little voice.

Which he ignored. "I wake up at dawn because, for me, that's the best time for my writing. It's the time when my brain functions best. And I keep at it, locked into my study, until afternoon. I don't answer phones, I don't receive visitors. And, in the afternoon, after lunch, I often go back to work again. Or I go for long, solitary walks." He smiled faintly. "And that's my life, these days. Perhaps you'd call me a hermit; I'd say I'm a satisfied man."

"Is your farmhouse in a beautiful place?" Even she heard the wistful note in her voice.

"Oh yes, it is. I'm surrounded by deep woods, rolling hills, and there's a wild river down in the hollow. But in winter, I can be snowed in for weeks. And even in summer, the calm would drive some people crazy." He stopped.

They sat in silence for a long while.

"Felicity?"

"Yes?" Her heart pounded slowly, then stopped beating altogether. What was he going to say? That they could give it a try? That she could come home with him, see what it was like? That he wanted her to love the hills, the forest, the animals, and insects as much as he did? That it just might work between them this time around? Because it would. She knew it would.

"Don't you see?" he said gently. "Don't you see what would happen? To the two of us? Again. We both know my days in solitary confinement would drive you crazy. We've already been down this road—or one very similar. One day we'd be loving each other, and the next you'd be leaving me again, running off to the next flood, the next Pakistani water-pump detail, the next civil war, the next far away place where you can lend a helping hand, and experience the noisy, busy world."

"It's not true. I've retired from that now." She was certain of it, too. And now it was time she told him what her plans were, what she'd been dreaming about doing for so long now. About settling down. Finally. Writing a book.

"It's your turn now. Tell me about your love life," he said, cutting into her thoughts. "What about the other men you've known? You must have had other relationships in your life, even though you were in dangerous places. You must have met many interesting people."

"Sure. As an aid worker you meet an incredible amount of people—interesting ones and less interesting ones. You meet locals in the countries where you're living, and you meet other expatriates. But even if you're surrounded by men and women all the time, you live with a constant feeling of loneliness because you're always on the move. For most workers, the maximum contract length in any one place is two years, but in really dangerous places—Afghanistan, Central Africa, South Sudan—you're only there for six months. So you end up with friends and lovers in Pakistan, or Iraq, or Mali, or Zimbabwe, but you've never spent more than a few months with any of them."

"Pakistan? Zimbabwe? Mali?" Marek shook his head. "Listen to you. We're so different, Felicity. I hate traveling. For me, going into New York is a wild, nerve-rattling voyage I'd rather avoid. And right now, I'm glad we got this chance to see just how different we really are. The memory of you has stayed with me for all these years, like a bone stuck in my craw. I always wondered where you were, what you were doing, and if we couldn't have made our relationship work, after all."

A sudden wave of anger and frustration wrenched her out of his arms and onto her feet. She stood in front of him, her eyes blazing. "Stop beating around the bush, Marek. Just be open and honest. You can't be bothered trying again. That's what it is. You're afraid, so you're protecting yourself as best you can."

"That's probably true, too," he said slowly, his voice steady, calm, sure. He stared at her, feasted his eyes on her, took her in like a man in need of a breath of fresh air. Now that their time together was coming to an end. "But I'm not beating around the bush. Don't you see the sense in what I'm saying?"

"No. I don't."

"I'm doing this for both of us. I'm showing you that loving someone is also letting that person go free. Free to pursue their dreams. I'm simply pointing out the obvious."

"And stop pushing out those stupid, worn-out old clichés at me!" Felicity railed. She felt like stamping her foot or punching the wall. The arrogance of the man. Brushing her off. And he wasn't even brave enough to admit it. "So that's it, eh, Sumner? I love you. You love me. It's been great. So long?"

"There's no future for the two of us as a couple. Can't you leave it at that?"

"No!" It was an explosion. Hell! She was begging again. Begging, because what he was saying hurt so much. Standing here, naked as the day she was born, and begging, and feeling foolish. And desperate.

She turned, raced into the cabin. Clothes. She had to get some clothes on her body. Add a little dignity to the situation or, at least, put on a protective wall.

She was yanking an Indian print dress over her head when she heard him come in.

He was leaning against the door jam, his silhouette lit by the bright glare of the sky flashing against the background of sea. Like a god, tall, and muscular, and beautiful, and not for her to possess.

"I'm trying to avoid hurting you more than necessary. Or hurting myself," he said gently.

"Because this doesn't hurt now?" She gazed at him with despair.

"It shouldn't."

"Oh, really? And just why is that?" She lifted her chin, defied him. "Because in your neat little world, people can give themselves totally and then walk off with no scars?"

"I wish I could tell you there's hope. I wish I could bring you home with me. But those are only wishes and I can't. It won't work. Not for me, not for you. But we'll see each other again. We'll keep in touch from now on. Write to each other. Call. That's the best way for the two of us."

Then, all the fight went out of her. She felt her shoulders sag with defeat. Her voice was bitter because she knew she'd done her best. Played her wild card and lost.

"It's always been like this between us, hasn't it? I make the first moves. You follow, intrigued, for a while. And then, you quit."

"Exactly what I'm trying to tell you. I'm a loner. I'm inflexible. What's the use of saying we'll commit to something that won't work on a daily basis? Not in the long run, it won't."

"Well, get this into your head, Sumner. It's started again, our relationship. Our couple. We started the whole thing way back in the 1970s, and we restarted it a few days ago. Now. When you brought me back to that hotel room of yours. When you slept beside me the whole first night. When you brought me that rose. And you know what? You're going to dream about these days we've spent together. You're going to dream about me night after night. And you're going to hate yourself for running away."

Her passion touched him. Very much. But not quite enough to want to take the risk.

"Perhaps you're right, Felicity. Perhaps."

"I know I am." But how could she know what would happen in the future? She could only hope the next step—undeniably his—would be taken.

****

There were bad moments in life and there were worse ones. This was one of the worst. *You'll get over this one day, Felicity*, she told herself for the thousandth time, and with diminishing conviction. People always got over broken hearts. Even broken hearts that felt this bad? She wasn't so sure. She hurt so much, she was almost cramped over in her seat. Even the landscape seemed to mirror her despair. Rolling hills bleached yellow by the sun, dust, the glare of a too-blue sky.

The real world had finally intruded: they had left paradise behind. Marek had telephoned his agent, and now they were driving back up north, in the direction of the airport. In a few hours time they'd be forced to smile and say, "Good-bye" and "Great seeing you again. Take care of yourself."

They planned to leave the rented car at the airport. Marek would catch a plane to Boston; he was meeting his son there, and they were going off for a week together—it had been planned months before. After that, he'd be speaking at a university somewhere. Taking up his busy life again.

Well, life is just fine and dandy for some folks.

"What are your plans?" Just like that, he was asking her. As if she were just stepping around the corner to buy a new hat or some chewing gum. Why had she ever thought she loved him? No, she had to change that around. She *knew* she loved him, but she would do her very best to stamp out the feeling. Block out the rush of sentiment, the caring and the hope.

"Oh me. You know how restless I am. You haven't stopped pointing it out to me since we've been together." She waved her hands in an airy little gesture to show people of her ilk didn't plan. They just did. "I'll probably jump on a plane to Germany—if I can find one that's leaving today. Go pick up my clothes at my friend Maria's apartment, then head east. Maybe go to Hungary."

"Hungary?" He turned slightly and stared for as long as the traffic would allow. "This is the first time you've mentioned Hungary. What are you going to do there?"

As if she knew. She'd just rattled off the name of the first country she could think of. What indeed would she do there if she decided to really go?

"Learn Hungarian, of course." She knew she was sounding so superficial, but she didn't care one whit.

"Hungarian? What for?"

Good question. "Why not?" *Scrape your thoughts together.* "You see, I'm one of the lucky ones in the world these days. I don't really have to do anything if I don't want to. I can go learn Mandarin Chinese if I've a hankering to do so. If I'm frugal enough. I have a little money, so I'll always be all right."

He still knew so little about her. About the way she was feeling right now, for example. For someone who'd made such grand declarations of love, for someone who'd shown such intensity of feeling over the last few days, she was now looking incredibly impersonal.

And it hurt. He didn't know why it hurt as much as it did. He'd been the one who'd pointed out they had no future together. That they couldn't live together. That he didn't want permanent commitment in his life. So why did it bother him so much that she didn't seem to care anymore? That she'd stopped fighting?

"And you? What are your plans after you get home? Will you be getting right to work on a new book? Or do you have to do research?"

"Let's just say I'm turning ideas around in my head at the moment." He didn't feel like elaborating. The closer they got to the airport, the less happy he was feeling.

"Marek. About being a writer..." she began timidly. "Do you think there are particular subjects that won't interest the public at all? That no publisher would be interested in either—not that you have that problem, of course. You're in the lucky position of being able to write exactly what you want. You have a big name."

"A big name." His short laugh was humorless. "That's not always an advantage. I can't begin to tell you how many people run after me because they want to be associated with my big name. And those with no talent who want me to influence publishers and agents on their behalf. And let's not forget all the folks who look me up because they too want to write a book one day, and they need my help."

She'd stopped breathing, felt her blood run cold: *people who look me up because they too want to write a book one day and need my help?* That's what he'd said, wasn't it?

Oh, hell! What if she'd told him she'd also been planning to write a book. A book about all the things she'd seen and experienced. Would he think she'd suddenly appeared on the scene again because of the help and influence he could give her? That she'd slept with him for that reason only? How humiliating.

He must never know. Never. Because if things had turned out differently, if he *had* wanted her to stay with him, that would have meant giving up on the idea of writing. Giving up a dream. It was exactly the same choice she'd been forced to make forty years earlier.

So now it really and truly was over. She could never have a happily-ever-after fairytale life with Marek.

Unless she somehow managed to be successful. Write the book of the year. On her own. Without him knowing what she was doing. Then she'd show him, all right.

If she got the chance.

****

The airport was filled to cracking with squalling babies, almost hysterical mothers, and exasperated fathers. Remote looking people in suits and holding attaché cases sought desperately to detach themselves from the general chaos.

"Will you really write to me?" Felicity asked flatly. She told herself she wasn't experiencing *déjà vu*. They'd already had this very same discussion years ago. And this time too, it was Marek running away. And this time too, she was off to pursue her own dream.

"I said I would. Why would I break my promise?"

"No. You won't write." She knew he wouldn't. "You didn't last time."

"Last time? Last time I actually made the effort to come to Paris, remember?" He raised a sardonic eyebrow.

"And you hated it."

He grimaced. "Do we have to go over all this again?"

"Okay, just forget it."

"Felicity?" He reached out for her chin, forced her to meet his eyes. "This isn't the end. We'll meet up again, okay? Please, keep in touch with me. We'll plan some time together. But for the time being, let's just think about what we've shared. Let's get the experience straight in our heads."

Did he really mean what he'd said about meeting up again? She doubted that, too. He was just trying to soften the blow. He'd been so cool, so removed ever since they'd left the cabin.

"Look," she said. "I'll give you an address where you can reach me if you want. An address in Germany. Maria, my friend, always forwards my mail on to me. So I *do* get it. Eventually." She was talking too quickly. Even she could detect the faint note of hysteria in her voice. Pulling a scrap of paper out of her purse, scrabbling around for a pen, she hoped he didn't notice how badly her hands were shaking. If only time would pass more quickly. This was horrible, this situation. Both of them embarrassed, and kicking their heels here in the lobby of the airport.

"You don't have an Internet address?"

She looked at him. Blinked. "An Internet address?"

"And no cell phone, of course." He laughed, shook his head. Of course not. He reached for his wallet, fished out a card, handed it to her. "My home address in Connecticut. If you need anything, call me." Something in his eyes told her there was something else he wanted to say but couldn't.

She heard his flight being called over the loudspeaker.

"Felicity—"

"Don't!" She held up her palm, in warning.

"Don't what?"

"Don't say 'It's been great.' I can't bear hearing that." She grimaced.

"I wasn't going to." His face was drawn, his eyes unsmiling.

"Fine." She wasn't going to cry either. No way.

"*Au revoir.*"

Au revoir? Meaning "See you again"? Or had he really meant to say, "*Adieu.*" Meaning goodbye forever.

He bent down, touched her lips with his, the caress of a warm summer's breeze, soft, gently loving, and just as transient.

Chapter Twelve

"Damn!" Felicity kicked the offending iron stove with her foot and was instantly sorry she'd done so. Her toes hurt like hell. "Damn again!" When things went wrong, they did it with a vengeance. It had been raining for three days solid. Her room was freezing cold, and this was only October. She'd tried lighting the coal-burning stove, and it smoked. Then went, damply, out. She'd been sitting on a granite-hard chair all day trying to write, and she hated the result. She hated herself at the moment and most of all she hated Marek Sumner, that shadowy figure who was on the other side of the world, in Connecticut. She hated him because she couldn't get him out of her mind, and that was making her miserable.

Still, she'd done all she could do, hadn't she? She'd gone running after him. She'd tracked him down, chased him, seduced him, and given him all the love it was possible to give another human being. And where had it gotten her?

To the airport. To Hungary. Then to this place: a backwoods village in the east of the country. A village of half-paved roads, low-lying houses, and barking dogs, perched on the edge of an endless plain of dried-out sunflowers. A place where she couldn't understand a word anyone said. Trying to write a book, but not being certain she had enough talent for the task.

If that wasn't complete failure, she didn't know what was.

If only she could stop thinking about Marek. If only she could get him out of her mind for one whole minute of the day, that would at least be something. But she couldn't. All the silly, banal, meaningless moments they'd passed together marched through her head over and over again, and she couldn't mastermind them back out again.

If she ate breakfast, she remembered what it had been like sitting across the table from Marek, in the Dew Drop Inn, five miles out of Island Park, eating eggs and toast and drinking a thousand cups of coffee while he told her about his books, the research he'd done, the quirky people he'd met, the different ideas for new work.

If she so much as swatted at an autumn-drowsy fly, she remembered sitting with Marek and Jep, the weak orange light of the kerosene lamp playing across the table, the squat glass of nasty jipple on the table in front of her.

"One thing good about California," Jep had said. "Don't got no flies."

And, looking over at her, Marek had sent her that secret, dancing smile of his.

And when she lay in her narrow wooden bed at night (the sheets damp, cold, and heavy from the sodden air) she remembered what it had been like to lie in Marek's arms, and her body ached so badly for his touch, for his warmth, for the sound of his even breathing, that she thought she'd go mad.

And, worst of all, she craved the sound of his voice. Would she ever be able to go through one whole day again without conjuring up the memory of his low, husky voice in her ear? Would she ever be able to banish the erotic promises he'd whispered when she'd lain in his arms? Those nights they had spent together, the tenderness he'd shown! Over forty years ago, what they'd shared was erotic discovery. Six weeks ago, Marek had shown her extreme gentleness could be so beautifully mixed with intense passion.

What had he left her with? A glimpse into what it would be like to be loved and cherished by him forever. The one thing that was impossible, that was making her suffer so much now.

Of course, no one had ever said a seven-night stand with the man you deeply loved would leave no scars. But they hadn't said how bad the aftermath would feel either. And Marek would never be able to imagine how much she hurt. He'd called her strong—whatever that meant. Because he'd wanted to have a good conscience when they separated? Because he didn't want to have to worry about her? Well, phooey on that. Strong people could hurt, too. And being strong also meant being strong enough to lean against a firm shoulder—the shoulder of the person you loved. Being strong enough to give yourself up to love.

She'd made one last, tiny effort. She'd sent him a postcard. Which he hadn't answered…naturally. That had been almost three weeks ago. She'd practically been hanging on the rusty mailbox for the last ten days, hoping for an answer which never came. It was adolescent behavior, she knew, and it wasn't even well-adapted adolescent behavior. The thought made her ashamed of herself.

Phooey on you, Felicity Powers. You'll be sixty-

J. Arlene Culiner

four years old in two weeks. You've been doing exactly what you want your whole life long, and you've done it on your own steam. You are tough, independent, and you don't need anyone in the world. Much less Marek Sumner, the man who obviously doesn't need—or want—you either.

How many times a days did she repeat those words to herself? Around a hundred. If she kept it up for the next year or two, or three, or six, she might even start believing them.

At least you can try and enjoy yourself. What was the choice?

She looked out the window. The rain seemed to have let up for the time being and the night was creeping in. What did you do for fun in this village? You went to the local bar run by Irinka, a huge, blowzy brunette who managed, single-handedly, to maintain order and respectability in a place that barely recognized such strange principles. Felicity shoved her feet into a pair of walking boots, threw a damp-feeling cardigan over the three other layers of sweaters she was already wearing, and headed out down the road. At least Karci might be in Irinka's. He was nice. She was even able to communicate with him to a certain extent—in pigeon German. He could give her another lesson in Hungarian. She'd pretty well managed to just about remember three words already.

Damn! Even her language skills seemed to have vanished in smoke. That experience with Marek Sumner in California had rendered her temporarily incapable of undertaking anything more intellectual than tying and untying her shoelaces.

****

194

It was going to be a wild goose chase, he was absolutely convinced of it. Marek was already regretting what he'd let himself in for—or he almost was. He thought of reasons why he shouldn't be doing it at all: it was out of character; there was the definite possibility of defeat hanging heavy on the horizon, and he hated defeat. Still, Felicity hadn't left him any choice. She'd left her image so deeply embedded in his mind, it was going to take him a hell of a lot longer than forty years to burn it out this time.

Since he'd seen her again, life without her had become impossible. The silence he loved, the isolation he'd craved, no longer made any sense to him. Being with Felicity had given life new meaning. All he had to do was sit on his back porch in Connecticut, stare out at the tangle of trees standing still in the Indian summer morning, and he'd find himself wondering what Felicity would think about the view. The day he received an invitation to a gallery opening in New York (aligned yellow raincoats instead of red bricks), he knew if Felicity were with him, he might even enjoy himself if he went. What would she think about the autobiographical manuscript he was working on? What would she say about the image of the San Francisco of the sixties and seventies he'd painted in too-nostalgic words? He needed her critical look at things.

What would it be like to wake up with Felicity every single morning for the rest of his life?

Fine. It would feel just fine.

What if every day was a battle of wits?

So what? Isn't that what life really should be?

What if waking up with her meant living in a hut in Mongolia? Or in Niger? With nothing but a dark plain and jagged rocks stretching out as far as the eye can see?

Well, why not. If Felicity can manage, so can I.

And no shower. No breakfast in sight. No comfort, no central heating, no washing machine, no electricity. No place to charge the laptop or the cell phone, no plug for the printer or the fax.

So what? Why did he need electricity? He wasn't going to be a slave to technology! He could always dig out an old portable typewriter, couldn't he?

He tried to imagine sitting with Felicity in some hopeless desert highlighted by a glowing sunset. They would be roasting unidentified, charred bits of matter over a sickly fire. There would be no water, no security, no elegant bottle of wine, no fame, no fortune.

It sounded fine.

Because he loved her. Because, despite all those intervening years, he knew her as well as he knew the back of his hand, and even better than his own soul. She'd been right, accusing him of being a coward. He'd been too afraid to make their relationship work. He'd been so afraid of getting hurt, he'd forbidden himself to try. And even worse than being a coward, he'd been a fool. A fool who'd run away because he'd met his opposite. A fool who hadn't recognized being with an opposite meant life would always be stimulating. Exciting.

And he'd let Felicity, his opposite, get away. Again.

Images of the beach in Island Park came back to him, Felicity stretched out in the sand, naked, laughing up at him. Then telling him she loved him. He wanted to have the experience again. With Felicity. For the rest of his life. Everything would be wonderful, just as long as they did it together. He had to tell her. He'd hurt her; he had to make up for the pain he'd caused her.

As quickly as possible…if he ever found her.

There was no way of reaching her by phone. Fax was out of the question. She probably lived hundreds of miles from an e-mail connection, and she might not know what that was anyway. He didn't even have a normal address for her or, at least, not a useful one. Oh yes, there was the stamp on the postcard she'd sent him: Magyarorszag. That definitely meant Hungary (and why couldn't Hungarians use the same name for their country everyone else did?) Then there was the postmark. Kunkisörs—wherever that might happen to be.

One postcard was all he'd had to go on. One postcard received two weeks ago. And in Felicity's flamboyant handwriting: "I think about you so often, it's almost as if you're here with me."

No heading. No signature. A coded message, beckoning him. Unless he was totally mistaken. Unless he'd gotten it all wrong, something—where Felicity was concerned—that was totally possible.

He'd consulted his atlas: no luck. Bought a detailed map of the country and searched for a place name resembling—however slightly—Kunkisörs. And he'd found it. A tiny dot way out in the middle of nowhere, not so far from the Ukrainian border. The flat, empty puce-colored expanse of the map told him nothing of any respectable size lay in the vicinity. He sighed. When Felicity wanted to disappear, she did it in a big way.

Budapest had been hell from the minute he'd

stepped off the plane. Trying to make himself understood was another trial. How the hell did you pronounce Kunkisörs in Hungarian? He felt everyone had been looking at him with hostility. They seemed determined, if he were to reach his destination, it would certainly be without their help. If he'd been superstitious, he'd have taken that as an evil omen. As it was, he forced himself to fight down superstition, tooth and nail.

How would Felicity handle this? That question came creeping into his mind—and not for the first time either. Well, if people were hostile, Felicity would probably just shrug, or even smile. Charm everyone and get what she wanted after all. He didn't have Felicity's ease—it would take him years to accumulate that—but the shrug was easy enough.

But why, in heaven's name, were there so many train stations in Budapest! At least three of them. And he'd ended up going to two of the wrong ones before finding the right—and the experience only reminded him why he'd always hated traveling...although with Felicity, things were bound to be easier.

And here he was. On a small trunk line, in an ancient, ill-sounding train, rattling and swaying its lazy way through a flat, autumnal countryside. A countryside without incident, without accent. Tall acacias, reedy swamps, fields turning yellow and red in the waning afternoon light. At every stop he had to stick his head out of the loose, clattering window and peer around for the barely visible station names. No question of anyone announcing the stops, of course, and he wouldn't have been able to understand what they said anyway.

Now, with an exhausted scream of brakes, the train came to another distressed halt. He jammed his head out of the window once again. Yes, this was it. A faded sign under the hanging roof of a lopsided verandah declared this to be Kunkisörs.

He stepped out.

Reeds waved in the chilly breeze. From the window of the shabby station, he could see a curious face watching him. He was the only one to descend. Naturally. Here again were only acacias, fields, and weeds. Why would anyone come to a place like this? The air was so damp, it fogged his glasses. Certainly there must be a town. Somewhere. He headed away from the station. No point in even thinking about asking for directions. He was going to have to play this by ear—or instinct, whichever insured his survival.

Etched on the far horizon, he saw the steeple of a church. That must be Kunkisörs. Shouldering his bag, he headed down a rather indecisive-looking road. Low houses crouched sullenly here and there, became more plentiful but not more welcoming. Yes, he definitely was heading in the direction of civilization—or what passed for civilization in this part of the world. He, himself, was starting to feel as if he'd just stepped off a flying saucer. The odd inhabitants of the place seemed to think so also. They came out of their houses to stare unabashedly and unsmilingly.

"Good evening," he called out. No one bothered to answer.

"*Guten Abend.*" It was the limit of his German. They still didn't answer. His shoe soles made soft, lonely, tapping noises on the road. From time to time he could hear the lowing of invisible cows. The sky had darkened considerably. It even looked like rain was imminent. He hoped there would be a hotel or even a small pension in the center of town.

A vain hope. There wasn't one. As far as he could see, there wasn't even a center. Damn Felicity! How would he find her? Who could he ask? Perhaps she wasn't even here? The thought chilled him, and he pushed it out of his mind. If she wasn't here, if she'd gone off somewhere else, Madagascar or Tahiti or Tibet, what would he do then? He'd forget her. For forever.

If he could.

But right now? Well, he'd try and find a restaurant, mention Felicity's name. If she was gone, he'd settle down for a good meal and a beer or wine—whatever they served here. Then try and beg someone to rent him a back room, or an attic, or a tent, or a dry barn to sleep in. Head the hell out of here in the morning. All of that, and in that order.

He stopped. The road had opened up into a main square. Aside from the square shape and the fact it was obviously a crossroads, there wasn't anything main about it. Across the road, was the church. To the north, south, east, and west were simply more of the same low-lying houses. He saw curtains twitch and knew he was still being watched.

Damn Felicity and the hold she had on him!

Okay. No hotel, no pension, no restaurant, no stores here either. So now what? There must be another train out of this place. He could just turn around and head back in the direction of the station. *Go on. Do just that,* whispered his personal insidious little voice from the dark, defeated regions of his mind. *She'll never have to know you've been here.*

A bar. At least there had to be a bar. Somewhere. He looked around desperately.

A dozen children had gathered on the far side of the square and were now huddled together, giggling and watching him. What was so funny? An ancient codger, leaning against a bicycle, chewing slowly, made no effort to disguise the fact he was gaping.

Marek marched over to the man, stared into his misty blue eyes.

"Do you speak English?"

The man stopped chewing. Stared back. Began to chew again.

"German?"

Nothing.

"Is there a bar here? Bar. Bar..." It was time for pantomimes, evidently. He imitated a man drinking a glass of beer.

Comprehension dawned along with a snigger of complicity. Crooking a finger, the old fellow motioned for Marek to follow him.

There was a bar, after all. The finger pointed down a back street. There, in the dusk, Marek could make out a red, black, and white sign shivering in the wind. A beer would be fine, would even be wonderful. Maybe there would even be peanuts. Hadn't he heard somewhere you could survive quite nicely on beer and peanuts for an incredible amount of time? The way things were looking now, he was about to test the mettle of that unlikely-sounding theory.

The light streamed past the net-curtained windows of the bar. So the place was open. He could even see moving shapes in there—people, most likely—although you had to be prepared for anything in life. Perhaps someone spoke English, although he also knew how hopeless that wish was. In any case, if Felicity Powers were anywhere in the vicinity, a local could help him find her. You couldn't help but notice someone like Felicity. Certainly here, you couldn't. Not in a place where peeking through windows seemed to be the national sport.

He pushed open the wooden door of the bar. And came to a dead halt.

She was there. In blue jeans and a lumpy sweater, her silvery hair an exciting tumble. Felicity.

As if this were the most obvious place in the world for her to be.

Perched, perjink, on a stool at the bar. Laughing at something someone was saying. Until she looked over in the direction of the open door, saw him, and froze. Until an expression of disbelief mixed with wonder flooded over her face.

Easy to read, she'd always been easy to read. Couldn't fool an earthworm, Felicity couldn't.

"Marek?" It was a gasp.

He noticed the tall, too handsome, muscular, mustached man standing by her side at the last moment. Oh no. Shades of Paris? An army of admirers to be fought through? He wasn't feeling very much like a warrior.

"Marek!" She'd found her voice. "What are you doing here? Why are you in Kunkisörs? How did you get here?" She swallowed, shook her head slowly. Blinked. "I mean, this place isn't just a little meander down the road from Connecticut. It's a whole journey."

"Guess it is." His mouth was twitching. "Actually,

I just popped in to say hello. And have a beer."

"Well, you don't say," she said faintly. "Only…" She stopped. Looked puzzled. "I must admit I'm having the sudden but very distinct feeling I've been dropped into a dream world, or at least into another dimension. And I'm not having much luck working out what's going on. Unless…Unless you're here for me."

He felt like roaring with laughter. But managed to keep cool. "Could be, you know."

"Uh huh. But you're not looking very friendly. Not really. Uh…Marek?" She turned slightly pink. Slipping off the bar stool she took two steps in his direction. Hesitated. "Hey, listen. Would it be all right if…I mean would you mind awfully if I threw my arms around you? I mean, just to make sure you're real?"

"I'm real enough, and that sounds just fine to me. If the brute at your side gives you the okay."

"Brute?" Felicity turned slightly. Then remembered she wasn't sitting alone. She began to giggle. "Oh, this is Karci. He's teaching me Hungarian."

"I'll bet he is." Marek could just imagine the sort of vocabulary Felicity was learning with someone who looked like Karci.

"Marek, don't start." Three steps more and she was standing right in front of him, a hair's breadth away. Still, she didn't move. Didn't put her arms up. "Marek? If I hug you, are you going to hug me back? Or are you going to take this as an imposition?" The situation was definitely gaining in absurdity.

"What kind of crazy question is that?" He dropped his bag to the floor, reached for her, pulled her into his arms and held her so tightly clamped against him she could feel the steady thud of his heart. For enchanted minutes the real world disappeared around her. She only knew this was where she wanted to be, that the rich musky scent of his skin was what she'd been dreaming about and missing so terribly over the last six weeks.

When he murmured her name, so quietly it was almost a whisper, she smiled and leaning back, looked up at him with passion-filled eyes. Yes, he really was here. This tall man with salt and pepper hair, and the green gaze warming her through and through.

"I love you, Marek," she said huskily.

"I know. I don't know what I did to deserve it though."

"You're here. That's enough." It was. It was the biggest declaration of love she could ever imagine. She wanted to tell him that. She also wanted to tell him she needed him, joyously, wonderfully. The very thought stunned her. She, tough-as-old-boots Felicity *needing* somebody? Age must have softened her up.

Stop hanging on him. Play it cool, for once.

She had to force herself to step back out of the embrace. All the eyes in the bar were focused on the two of them. Especially on Marek who stood there, grinning down at her with a very satisfied expression on his face.

She told herself she had to act normal. Casual. Or, at least she had to try. She was frightened of scaring him off with her intensity. "You want something to drink?"

"What's the local specialty?"

"Prune alcohol. Very strong. I wouldn't recommend it. Try a beer instead."

"And food?"

She grinned. "Another specialty. Sauerkraut soup. Mixed with the most evil red peppers anyone has ever conceived of."

He winced. "Come to Kunkisörs and die."

****

"So. This is the place you call home," said Marek, looking curiously around the white-washed, rough-walled room.

"I know what you're thinking," began Felicity defensively.

"Good. Be a sweetheart and tell me what it is."

"Don't be supercilious," she warned.

"Cold in here."

She sniffed. "The damn stove smokes and goes out every time I try to heat the place up."

"You need a man about the house." He glowered. "Or doesn't Karci run to such things as fire lighting."

"You've got a thing about Karci—"

"Me? I'd think he's more your style than mine."

"You know perfectly well what I'm saying. Karci is a friend—or would be if we could talk about things more complicated than the weather and the price of pickles."

"I thought he was teaching you Hungarian."

"He's trying," she said miserably. "You can't imagine how complicated Hungarian is. It's not an Indo-European language. It's Finno-Ugric, like Finnish and Estonian." She stopped. Why was she defending herself? Why were they even talking about this?

"Marek?"

He'd been prowling through the room taking in little details. The tiny double windows keeping out the wet, cold night. The old pieces of furniture, the polished planks on the floor. The papers scattered across the writing table, and covered with her own fantastic handwriting.

"Yes?"

She cleared her voice. "Did you come all the way here from Connecticut to talk to me about Karci? Or is it Hungarian grammar that really interests you?"

"Now who's being supercilious?"

"Supercilious? Me? I'd say the word *confused* was better suited to the occasion."

"What are you confused about?" He was smiling faintly.

"Look, I never did like playing cat and mouse games. Why don't you just clue me in?"

"About?"

Drawing on every single bit of her courage, she crossed the room and placed herself directly in front of him. "Marek, what are you doing here?"

He looked down at her, examining her eyes, her mouth, the finely drawn brows, the arch of cheekbones, the silvery cloud of hair tumbling from its usual messy chignon. He wondered how he could have let her go, back there in California. How he could have fooled himself into thinking he could do without her? He loved her. He wanted her. Simply those two things. Oh yes, there was also a third. He wanted her to feel the same way about him and back in Island Park he'd been so sure she had. But now? Did she still feel like that? After the way he'd treated her?

She was scowling up at him, he saw. It wasn't exactly the way he expected a woman in love to look. In fact, she couldn't have looked less like a woman in love than she did now. She looked more like an Amazon, a beautiful Amazon getting ready to go into battle.

"Make love, not war, Felicity."

She blinked. "What is this? Are we back to rehashing the sixties?"

"No way. And I think it should be perfectly obvious to you what I'm doing here. I'm here to rehash what happened six weeks ago." He paused. *Oh, out with it, Sumner*, he ordered himself. "Okay. I came here to tell you how much I love you."

"Oh. And? A postcard saying the same thing would have done the trick." She wasn't going to let herself hope. Not where Marek was concerned. That way she wouldn't be disappointed when he got on a plane and went back home again.

"And to show you I'm capable of making changes."

"What changes?" Hope was welling up again, and she had to do her best to squash it down.

"Well, for one, I can change my concept of home." He was being vague, too vague and he knew it. "Look, what I'm trying to say is, I want to live with you. If you want to go to the Sahara, I'll go with you. If you want to live here in Kunkisörs, I'll do it with you, too. If you want to come back to Connecticut with me, I'll go along with that. Let's just do it together, all right?"

She gulped, stared.

If he'd hoped to see joy and pleasure cross her face, he was disappointed. For a minute her expression went completely blank. Then her eyes filled with tears. Tears? Felicity Powers never cried. Almost never, anyway. *Only when you bring her a rose. Or ask her to live with you.*

Now what had he said wrong? Everything, obviously.

"I can't," she whispered. "I want to. So much. But I can't do it."

"You can't do what?" The panic was rising. "Why can't you?" She was going to tell him she'd just gotten married to Karci. Or joined a nunnery and taken a vow of celibacy. Or was leaving for a one-person expedition to the Antarctic with no return ticket—although that was a problem they just might find a viable solution for. Or she'd enlisted in the foreign legion in which case he'd have to stop being a pacifist and enlist, too.

"Because," she said sadly. "It wouldn't work."

"Oh. If that's what's bothering you..." The worst hadn't come to pass. "Why wouldn't it work? Look, Felicity, I'm not too crazy about hearing my own stupid words thrown back in my face. I was wrong. I admit it. The fact is, it doesn't work without you."

"No. I mean it. It won't work. When I tell you why, you'll start hating me."

"When you tell me what?" He was getting scared again.

"What I'm doing here. In Kunkisörs."

Running a spy ring—although what anyone would find to spy on in Kunkisörs was a mystery—unless the recipe for sauerkraut soup was a heavily guarded secret? Contraband? In what? Acacia trees?

"Come on. Clue me in."

She took a deep breath. Well, might as well get it over with now. That way he could turn on his heel and walk out the door and still leave her enough time to spend the rest of the night crying. "I'm trying to write a book."

He stared. "A book?"

"That's right!" She wasn't going to chicken out now. She wasn't. If he even dared be scornful, she'd show him what he could do with scorn. "A book. About the things I saw. About all the people I met. About the stories they told me. About what it's like to live on a plain that floods out every year. About what it feels like not to be able to read and write and be forced to make a baby a year. About—" She waved her arms wildly.

"Great."

"Great? What do you mean great! Don't you go and patronize me, Sumner." She lowered her head, bull-like, ready for a charge.

"I'm not patronizing you. I really think it's a great thing to do. And you are perfectly capable of doing it."

"You think so?" She stood there, blinking at him, the wind and fight temporarily knocked out of her sails.

"Why did you think I wouldn't?"

"Because I'm encroaching on your domain, for one."

"*My* domain? I'm not the only writer in the world, thank God. What's the next reason?"

"How can you ever trust me?" she said miserably. "Remember what you said in California? About all the people who just look you up because they want to write a book, and need your help. About the people who want to use you for your influence. And look at me. I suddenly show up, out of the clear blue and…"

"And you think I'll accuse you of the same thing," he finished for her. He was grinning quite openly now.

"Well, I—" She stared. "You won't?"

Obviously words weren't going to work as well as

action. He reached out for her, just the way he'd been aching to do since he'd been alone here with her. Pulled her into his arms, wrapped her tightly against him, and began kissing her. Kissing the softness of her neck, the delicate space behind an ear, her eyelids, her forehead, and the warm pulsing vein at the base of her throat.

It worked like magic. He could always count on it. He felt her crowding closer against him, fitting the soft pliancy of her body as tightly to his as she possibly could. When he finally lowered his mouth to hers he could feel the fire start to glow in her just the way it always did when he touched her. It was wonderful, feeling the softness of her breasts against his chest and the warmth of her belly against his. He dropped his hands from her back and cupped them over her bottom, lifting her so she could feel what was happening to him.

"I want you, too," she whispered. "Right here, right now."

"Like you always did?"

Was he teasing her? "Like I always do."

He forced himself to pull back slightly so he was looking down at her, down into her lidded brown eyes where he read love, and desire, and the answer to a million of his questions.

"Felicity, do you really think a woman who wanted to use me for my influence could make love like you do? Could give herself the way you give yourself to me?"

She could only stare up at him, words having deserted her.

"Tell me we'll make every effort to stay together. Starting now."

"I can't. It's impossible." She didn't sound very

convinced. "It can't work. You'll hate my life. I'll hate yours. You were the one who said that. You were right, too."

He almost wanted to laugh. That was Felicity, all right. Stubborn to the end. Resisting even when she knew the fight had been lost.

Well, it was time for him to pull out the big guns—while he still had the strength to do it. Time to walk out the door again. It was going to be mighty hard.

She saw him clench and unclench his jaw. Saw him struggle, then saw his face go blank.

"Well. I'll wish you good night, then." He released her from his arms so abruptly she almost fell.

"Good night?" She gaped at him. "What do you mean?'"

"Just that. I'm off to find a bed for the night. A room. A pension."

"What?" She couldn't believe what she was hearing. This wasn't happening. It couldn't be happening. She would strip off her clothes, jump on him, rape him, if need be. "You're not getting out of this room, Sumner. You're spending the night with me. Right there. In that bed." Her finger jabbed the air in the direction of her little bed. It was just narrow enough for him to be obliged to hold her tightly in his arms all night long.

The corners of his mouth tugged themselves into an evil grin. "You remember the old story of *Lysistrata*, don't you?"

"The play by Aristophanes?" Felicity frowned at the sudden change of subject. "What the hell are you bringing that up for?"

"Go on. What's the play about?" His eyes were

twinkling, and he certainly didn't look like a man in distress.

"The women refused to sleep with the men until..." She gave way to an explosive little laugh of disbelief.

"Right." He laughed down at her in that smug superior way of his that she hated to admit she adored.

"And that's what you're going to do now?" She began to scowl.

"That's it. I'm going on strike. No more lovemaking, no kisses, no hugs, no touching at all. Not until you agree to my deal, of course." He casually strolled over to where he'd left his bag, swung it up onto his shoulder, and headed in the direction of the door.

If he didn't wipe the grin off his face she'd take a slug at him. "I hate you!"

He laughed.

She resisted the temptation to throw something at him. "Besides, there's no pension in Kunkisörs. There's no hotel, there's no room to rent, and there are no spare beds."

"So what? I'll sleep in a field or in a haystack for one night. It won't kill me."

"It'll rain." She flung up her hands in a gesture of frustration.

"I'm washable." He reached for the doorknob.

"I really do hate you!" She didn't sound very convincing. "Damn!" She collapsed onto a chair. "Okay, Sumner. What's the deal?"

"A forty-year trial period." His face was impassive.

"Forty years? I'm going to have to live with you for a whole forty years?" He watched her mouth as it softened.

"That's only for starters."

"It'll be hell, I'm warning you." Then her mouth curved out into a wide-open grin that shot warmth through every part of his body.

Relief flowed through him. He relaxed. Dropped his bag on the floor again.

"You're right," he said. "It will be sheer unadulterated hell. I can hardly wait." Then he began to laugh. "And it might be about as close to heaven the two of us are likely to get."

A word about the author...

Born in New York, raised in Toronto, J. Arlene Culiner has spent most of her life in England, Germany, Turkey, Greece, Hungary, and the Sahara. She now resides in a 400-year-old former inn in a French village of no real interest. Much to everyone's dismay, she protects all living creatures—especially spiders and snakes—and her wild (or wildlife) garden is a classified butterfly and bird reserve.

http://www.j-arleneculiner.com